GRAVE
SECRETS

SYLVIA McNICOLL

Stoddart Kids
TORONTO · NEW YORK

*We gratefully acknowledge the Canada Council for the Arts
and the Ontario Arts Council for their support
of our publishing program.*

Published in Canada in 1999 by
Stoddart Kids,
a division of Stoddart Publishing Co. Limited
34 Lesmill Road
Toronto, Canada M3B 2T6
Tel. (416) 445-3333   Fax (416) 445-5967
E-mail Customer.Service@ccmailgw.genpub.com

Published in the United States in 1999 by
Stoddart Kids,
a division of Stoddart Publishing Co. Limited
180 Varick Street, 9th Floor
New York, New York 10014
Toll free 1-800-805-1083
E-mail gdsinc@genpub.com

Distributed in Canada by
General Distribution Services
325 Humber College Blvd.
Toronto, Canada M9W 7C3
Tel. (416) 213-1919   Fax (416) 213-1917
E-mail Customer.Service@ccmailgw.genpub.com

Distributed in the United States by
General Distribution Services
85 River Rock Drive, Suite 202
Buffalo, New York 14207
Toll free 1-800-805-1083
E-mail gdsinc@genpub.com

Canadian Cataloguing in Publication Data

McNicoll, Sylvia, 1954–
Grave secrets
ISBN 0-7737-6015-6
I. Title.
PS8575.N52G72 1999   jC813'.54   C98-932525-3
PZ7.M36Gr 1999

Cover illustration: Sharif Tarabay
Cover and text design: Tannice Goddard
Computer layout: Mary Bowness

Printed and bound in Canada

For Christine Sallie, who invited us to dig
for the pool in her backyard.

Acknowledgement

The author would like to thank her faithful, talented workshop friends: Jim Bennett, Nan Brien, Steve Donnelly, Jeff Hulley, Cathy Miyata, Rachel Preston, Estelle Salata, Gisela Sherman, Lynda Simmons and Sue Williams for providing support as well as laughter and fun along the way.

Author's Note

In Cornwall, Ontario, backing onto a graveyard, there is a former group home with a swimming pool buried in the backyard. The pool was buried by a chain gang of convicts, presumably because of the complaints of the neighbors. The grass never grows quite right in this spot.

As for the ghosts, they are all imagined.

1

Like broken fingers reaching through the earth, the tombstones begged for something. Attention. Care. Another chance maybe. I leaned over the chain link fence separating our property from the graveyard. At one end an old stone hut stood guard. Keeping something out or in, I couldn't tell which. The oak trees along the side bunched their branches into fists that shook in the early evening breeze.

"How do you like it so far?"

My heart flip-flopped hard.

"Hello?"

Shading my eyes against the setting sun, I looked in the direction of the voice: a girl's. "Hi," I called, making out a tall shadowy figure. The last rays of the sun glowed around her head like a halo.

"You're the new neighbor?"

"Nicholas Dilon," I answered, stepping closer to the side fence so I could see her more clearly. Thin, with white-blond hair as straggly as late-summer grass, she smiled at me, a happy gap-toothed grin. The wind fluttered her long skirt around her like the petals of a flower. No, more like a weed.

"I'm Marian." She threw open her hands at the world. "So? Do you like it?"

"What every kid wants. A cemetery in their own backyard."

"I meant your new home."

I stared back at the towering monstrosity. Built out of brick the color of dried blood, it cast a long shadow over us even in the near-darkness. The windows, huge square eyes without curtains or blinds yet, appeared oily black. *I hate it.* The thought pounded in my head but I shrugged my shoulders. "It's okay."

Marian scratched at her shin for a second and then straightened again. "But the graveyard bugs you, right?"

I gazed back at those desperate fingers, some reaching upward, some bowed to the earth. *Another chance, another chance.* It was what our new house screamed for too. I shook my head, trying to clear the feeling. "Nah. Do you want to take a stroll through?"

Marian shivered as she stared at the cemetery, then she grinned again. "If you're with me I can."

I looked at her, puzzled. Wasn't she allowed to go in on her own? "Well, that was the idea."

She still hesitated. "Come over to my side first." She pointed to a hole in the fence.

"Sure." I crawled through to Marian's yard, then we both scrambled over into the cemetery.

Sprinting forward right after she'd landed, Marian crossed her arms and hugged herself as though she felt cold. "I don't come here alone. Do you believe in spirits?" She was looking back at me as though she wanted to measure something inside my head.

"Spirits?" I nearly bumped into her. "You mean like the souls of the dead wandering around?" I made a face. "Nah."

We strolled off the pathway to walk between the older tombstones. Bleached a dirty white from decades of sun, they were covered in places by a grey-green fungus that hid parts of the fading messages engraved on them. Marian hurried ahead.

"Hey, what's your rush?" I called. "Don't be afraid," I told her gently as I caught her arm. "We're going for a walk, remember?"

Marian looked around uncomfortably. "Can we just keep going?"

"Sure, only slower." My toe suddenly caught on something hard and I stumbled. "What's this?" I kicked back the grass around a flat rock. "Oh geez, I've been walking on someone's grave. See this? It says *Mother*."

Marian hesitated and then crouched down, gently exploring the grass next to the stone with her fingers. "Here's *Father*." She pushed away the blades for me to see.

I found another flat rock on the other side of *Mother*. "Here's *Son*."

"Oh no, here's *Baby*." Marian covered her mouth with her hand.

"The Willobys. It's all one family. Look at that monument. See — their names are listed." I pointed to a large, upright tombstone at the head of the flat rectangles we'd uncovered.

She stood up and slowly backed away. "It's so sad."

"Must have been a bad year for them. All four died in 1880." I was kidding around, but Marian's eyes were filling. "Come on," I said softly. "It was over a hundred years ago. They'd be dead of old age by now anyway."

Then I realized Marian wasn't looking at the flat stones anymore. Instead she stared back toward the main path where a lamb statue stood on a tombstone.

"Let's go over," I said.

Silently, she followed me.

> *Corey Fairchild 1985–1990*
> **Beloved son of Harold and Mary.**
> *Yea, though I walk through*
> *The valley of the shadow of death,*
> *I shall fear no evil:*

"Someone you knew?" I asked Marian when I finished reading the inscription and noticed a tear sliding down her cheek.

"No," she said hesitantly. "But he was only five years old." Marian stared at the lamb for a moment.

Then she closed her eyes. "Do you think he . . . Corey, was afraid when he died?"

"I don't know. Depends how it happened."

"He was so young and all alone. He must have been terrified."

"I thought you didn't know the kid. How come you're so sure he was alone?"

Marian opened her mouth to answer and then I could almost see it on her face. She decided to change what she was going to say. She swallowed. "You have to go there alone. To the valley of death, I mean," she finally answered.

I stared at her. *Pret-ty strange.* We moved on. Ahead on the path was a newer, rust-colored monument with a faded pink plastic wreath.

"Albert Dobroski. The Stick Lady's husband," she explained when she saw where I was looking. "He used to live over there." She pointed to a squat clapboard bungalow across the graveyard from her house.

"Stick Lady?"

"You'll know her when you see her." Marian strode away quickly.

"What's that newer one over in the far end?" I called to Marian as I rushed to catch up with her. "It has some dried flowers on it."

We reached the small black speckled stone all by itself in a corner.

Alexander Gresko
Born December 6, 1975, Died 1990
Pray for his soul

I pointed to the date. "Hey, this guy has the same birthday as I do. December sixth."

Marian wrinkled her forehead. "He used to live at your house back when it was the Home."

"The Home?" Something gripped at my insides.

"You didn't know? It was a place for boys who got in trouble, like a reform school. We moved next door after it shut down."

I stared at the grave. "Did he die in my house?"

"I don't know." Marian spoke quickly like an excited kid. "But I heard there's treasure buried in your backyard."

"Yeah, right! We could use some of that."

"Only nobody's ever tried digging for it." Marian paused for a second, her brow wrinkling. "Maybe I have that wrong."

I started wondering about Marian. What was with her?

She faced my house now. "I used to see the high school kids sneak into your place for their parties. That's why there were so many broken windows."

"I never saw any."

Marian didn't answer. We heard footsteps on the gravel behind us and turned around. From a gate off the yard of the squat clapboard bungalow, a hunched-up older woman approached. She wore a black beret over dry, mustard-colored hair. One hand clasped her brown jacket closed and the other held onto a carved wooden walking stick. All her fingers seemed to be covered with gold rings and heavy red stones. She stopped at what looked to be a fresh grave and unscrewed her stick, pulling out the handle part, a brass duck head.

Marian gasped. "The Stick Lady!"

A long blade flashed in the dying sunlight and without warning, the woman jabbed it into the grave. "Ah hah!" she shrieked.

Marian ducked down. "Let's go. Hurry, before she sees us."

"Is that you, Sasha?" Too late. The Stick Lady had sheathed the sword again and turned our way. "Thank God in heaven you are all right." She seemed to be speaking to me, her eyes squinting as though to make out my features better. Now she headed toward us.

I didn't know how to answer her. "Hi," I said when she was closer. I couldn't just ignore the woman.

Her whole face broke into a smile, all her wrinkles turning up with her mouth. "Hello." She reached out as if she wanted to hug me but when I didn't step forward, she dropped her arms. "Be a good boy, Sasha. I have so many chores to be done. Will you come over soon, please?"

"Ma'am?"

She started walking away, leaning heavily on her cane.

Marian tugged at my T-shirt sleeve. I yanked it back. "What's your problem?"

"She's a witch." Marian grabbed my sleeve again.

"Get off it." I was angry at her, that she was so afraid — but more angry that she'd made me afraid, too.

"She was talking to the corpse with her stick!"

Marian whispered. "And if you look now, she's talking to her husband."

"You believe that?" I turned and saw the Stick Lady kneeling in front of Albert Dobroski's grave. Sure enough, her lips moved. I glanced back at Marian.

Marian nodded once. Her eyes blinked rapidly and she tugged at my sleeve again.

"Let go of me!" I snapped at her. Her fingers opened and she shrank away. "That's better." I softened my voice. "Look, it's getting dark, we have to leave anyway."

We both walked more quickly toward the gate and out into the street, Marian staying quiet.

I started up a more ordinary conversation with her. "What school do you go to?"

"I'll be starting at Pearson in two weeks."

"No! I thought you were . . ." *Younger* was what I didn't say. She'd seemed so scared and unsure of herself. "I'm going there too."

We came up onto Main Street now. "Over there's the swimming pool." Marian pointed. "And over there's Donut King." She gave me her jack-o-lantern grin, her mood brightening. "I got my allowance today." She touched the pocket at the side of her skirt. "Want to have a donut? My treat."

I wasn't sure what letting her buy me a donut meant. Would we be best buddies from now on? She was too weird. I wasn't ready for that. "Uh, maybe some other time. I'd better get back to unpacking my things."

We turned up Winfield, our street. The other houses were small one-storey homes in assorted shades of aluminum siding. Only Marian's and ours towered up two stories.

The square-eyed windows of our house had been recently replaced, it was obvious to me now. The front door, a huge, red-brown wooden mouth, seemed open in a surprised square O.

"Nicholas?" Marian pleaded as we reached the concrete path to the mouth.

"Yeah?"

"Sometimes . . . at night . . . I see things." She grabbed at my T-shirt again. "Over at the graveyard, I mean." Her eyes scanned my face as though searching for something.

"Why are you telling me this?"

"Because . . . no one believes me. I know I'm different. I mean, I have trouble . . ." She hesitated, studying the ground for a moment. "I need extra help in school." Now she looked straight at me again. "But I still know when I see something. Don't you think I would?"

She looked anxious now and I felt sorry for her. "Of course. What kind of things?"

"A shape, just a shape. But I feel so strange when I see it."

"Maybe it's Old Lady What's-Her-Name."

"The Stick Lady?" Marian shook her head.

"Well then, it could be anybody. Anyone wandering the graveyard at night would look pretty spooky."

"But will you help me?" She looked around quickly.

"How?"

"Please, just let me know if you see things too."

2

"Don't go off mad!" Mom stomped up the stairs after me. "I just forgot to tell you."

I stopped on the landing outside my bedroom and looked back at her. "What else am I going to hear from our loony neighbors?"

Mom couldn't look me in the eyes. "Something happened here and that's why they shut down the Winfield Home."

"Something bad, right?"

Mom stared right at me. I could see all the new worry wrinkles around her eyes. "We ignored it because this house was all we could afford, Nicholas. Without it, your father could never have opened the business."

"What happened?" I asked more gently.

"Some kind of accident. It was years ago. That's all the real estate agent told me. I didn't ask for the details. I didn't want to know." Mom followed me into my room and stopped talking for a moment as she looked around. Now that it was time to sleep there, my bedroom seemed darker, dirtier. If this had been a motel, I know we would have driven away immediately.

"We should take before and after pictures," Mom said.

The olive green wall-to-wall rug was dotted with solid black circles — cigarette burns. My mattress lay slumped on top of it. The walls were smudged with dirt and one was streaked with something white. "Looks like pigeon droppings," I grumbled.

Mom smiled. "Pigeons don't fly sideways."

"Maybe they do here." I nodded at the smudge. "What is that then?"

"Your dad just primed a stain." She touched my shoulder lightly. "Don't worry, after we paint tomorrow, you'll never know it was there." She stared into space. Then she seemed to shake herself loose of her thoughts and forced another smile. "Sweet dreams, Nicholas. You know, they say the first dream you have in a new home will come true?"

"No, I never heard that one. I'll try to dream that my Ferrari is parked right outside, ready to take us away."

"You're too young to drive."

"In Alaska, I could at least have my learner's permit. We should have moved there."

Mom frowned.

"Just kidding. Listen, I'll try to dream that the house is all fixed up and fit for humans to live in."

"That's an idea." Mom's mouth twisted unhappily as she glanced at the white smears across the wall, then she turned and left the room. "Sleep tight."

"Don't let the bedbugs bite," I muttered automatically and shuddered. I have a thing about any kind of insects and this place looked like there might be plenty.

She shut the door gently. I took off my clothes and lay back on my bed, arms folded behind my head, staring at the ceiling. My arms and legs felt heavy but thoughts crackled through my mind like electricity. I couldn't get comfortable — on one side, on my back, over to my other side, onto my stomach. This was ridiculous. I tried the process backward. I bunched the sheets around me. Then I flung them away. Finally, I bolted upright. How long had I been lying there? I glanced at my watch: 12:15. At this rate I'd never fall asleep.

What now? I hate tossing and turning so I got up and walked over to my window to check out the view. Moonlight blanched the graveyard trees bone white. I slid back the window and the night breeze blew in a coolness as well as an unmistakable odor. It was a strong chemical smell — out of place somehow, but familiar, reminding me of pleasant experiences too. The scent of fun. Yet I felt cold, a deep damp chill, as though I'd suddenly fallen through ice.

Between the trees, I spotted a shape glowing. *Tell*

me if you see things, Marian had said. Well, this was definitely a thing. I didn't feel afraid, though, I felt something else — a strong curiosity. I wanted to climb out the window and go toward the shape.

I slid back the screen and stuck my head and upper body out into the night. I watched the shape intently. As though fixed in one spot by my attention, it hovered there. Was it watching me too? Why? Gradually my curiosity changed into something more powerful — a longing that wrenched at my stomach, giving me something close to pain. Why was I feeling this way? What or who was that figure?

The wind sighed through the trees and the leaves whispered back. The branches waved hypnotically. Rain began falling in a soft rustle. The shape finally moved, slowly floating along the graveyard fence, back and forth. Several times it stopped at Marian's side. At these times, my stomach hurt the most.

Then the wind moaned and the branches waved more frantically as the rain shushed them with a demanding rush. The shape slipped off between the trees again, but my stomach still hurt.

How long did I stand there watching the storm get worse and worse? I glanced at my watch; the numbers flashed 12:20. Only five minutes had passed, five minutes that had stretched on to eternity.

Thunder rumbled low and I turned my attention back outside. Lightning blitzed the sky, whitening it in brief flashes so that I could see the tree branches struggling to get loose. When did I go back to bed? I honestly don't remember lying down again.

I only remember running — running so hard that my blood pounded in my ears and my breathing turned ragged and desperate. Running to escape and running to get somewhere.

3

Something startled me awake. I'd managed to fall asleep after all. I felt exhausted but still wired with that strange electricity of last night. The nightmare gnawed at the pit of my stomach, promising to return and repeat itself if I fell back asleep.

Smelling Dad's coffee brewing, safe and inviting in the kitchen, I forced myself to get up, take a deep breath and follow the aroma. Off at the crack of dawn, Dad had left the pot on for Mom as usual. I grabbed a cup from a box, filled it halfway with coffee and the rest of the way with milk. The cup felt warm against my fingers and I held it in both hands for a moment, enjoying the soothing effect.

A small flickering shadow passed over the wall

above my head. Once, twice, three times. Finally I glanced toward the light to see what was making the shadow. *Hawh!* I jumped back.

Five or six wasps swarmed around it. Even while I watched, they were joined by another and then another, and at the window, more wasps bounced frantically against the pane. It was just too much.

Something touched my shoulder and I jumped back again. "Easy, Nicholas. It's only me." Mom peered at me through sleep-swollen eyes. "What's the matter?"

"Look over there!" I set my cup down and pointed up. Around the kitchen light and window an even larger swarm of wasps circled and buzzed.

Mom's eyes opened wide. She grabbed a broom and started whacking at them. "I see where they're getting in. Here, take this." She handed me the broom while she slammed down a window.

I stood frozen, staring first at all the wasp bodies on the floor, then at the live ones buzzing around.

"Snap out of it, Nicholas. Come on. Let's go into the living room."

I dropped the broom and grabbed my cup as Mom dragged me out. "I want to go back home. I hate this place," I said. When she let go of my arm, I stood there stiffly, shaking my head.

"Come on, Nicholas, they're just bugs. We'll eat breakfast out and everything will seem better after."

My hand shook as I went to sip my coffee again. "Ahhh!" I whipped the cup away from my lips, spilling the lukewarm liquid over my hand.

"What's wrong now?"

A lone wasp floundered on the surface of my coffee. Mom grabbed the cup from my hand and took it into the bathroom. I heard the toilet flush. "Get your jacket. Let's get out of here."

There was no more rumbling or white blitzes, but the sky looked sullen and bruised like it had lost a fight. A steady drizzle still came down.

When we reached Donut King, I tried to smile. "Maybe we could stay here till Dad gets home."

"You're such a wuss," Mom grinned at me. "We can't let a bunch of insects win."

We dashed across the lot into the shop.

Someone waved frantically at us from a booth near the window. "Nicholas, Nicholas! Over here."

I tried to duck behind Mom. "Don't look now. It's my new friend."

Mom sidestepped. "Stop that! We're going to be neighborly and sit with her."

"Whatever," I answered. It wasn't that I minded spending time with someone who was different when I had nothing better to do. But when school started, I didn't want to be joined at the hip to the neighborhood weirdo.

Mom strode over to Marian's booth. "Hi, I'm Nicholas's mother, Joanne. You must be Marian."

Marian grinned and nodded, sliding over in the booth. She patted the empty space beside her and Mom sat down there.

"Hi, Nicholas," Marian said brightly. "My mother's just getting another coffee over there. She'll be so excited to meet you."

A tall woman with a pink complexion and silver hair approached our booth, a cup in her hand.

"Mom, these are the new neighbors," Marian called, and waved at her. "Remember the boy I told you about?"

"Shhh, dear, we're in a public place," her mother told her.

Marian blushed and looked down.

I moved over so that Marian's mom could have her seat back.

She smiled a patient-looking smile and slid in. "Hello, I'm Wilhemina James. Doctor James. My friends call me Willy."

Mom shook the hand Willy extended. "Hi. Joanne Dilon. This is my son, Nicholas."

"We're very glad to have neighbors, I can tell you." Dr. James commented. "Aren't we, Marian?"

Marian's mouth was full of donut now but she nodded obediently.

"Living next door to an abandoned ... um ... that is to say, empty house doesn't do much for property value," Dr. Willy continued. "Although I don't envy you all the work that house needs. How did you get the graffiti off the walls? We could see it from Marian's bedroom window."

"Graffiti?" I stared Mom's way.

Mom winced, avoiding my eyes. "We covered it with primer."

The stain behind the pigeon droppings ... What kind of graffiti? I wondered.

Mom swallowed some coffee and then reached

over to touch my hand. "This afternoon, Nicholas and I will be painting over it all and we'll never have to think about it again."

"That's good." Dr. James paused and no one spoke for a moment. Then she started up the conversation again. "Well, it's certainly a very spacious house. The layout's the same as ours, you know."

Mom smiled. "Except every one of our doors and cupboards has it's own key. I must have a million of them. I guess they didn't trust the boys much."

"No. But they couldn't, could they? I mean those young people were all petty thieves of one sort or another."

Mom sipped at her coffee again. "All things said, I'm certainly glad to have the house."

Dr. James didn't recognize the expression on Mom's face and went on. "It's been empty for almost a year. No one wanted to live there. We bought our property at a reduced price, too."

"What were they scared of, ghosts or something?" I piped in, half-kidding. I didn't expect Dr. James' reaction.

"Marian's been talking to you, hasn't she?" The doctor glared at her daughter and Marian shook her head anxiously. Dr. James looked me over then. Her eyes were the same light blue as Marian's but there was a bright hardness in them. "Take my advice, Nicholas. Don't believe everything you hear. And don't let your imagination run wild. It won't help matters any."

Her eyes still gripped mine as though she needed to bend me to her will.

Mom cleared her throat, drawing attention away from me. "Well, Marian, what's there to do for young people in this neighborhood?"

Marian smiled gratefully. "The pool is just a couple of blocks away. I volunteer there some mornings. It's part of my lifesaving course. I'm at the third level, going for my certificate."

"That's great!" Mom said. "Nicholas would be about there too, if we hadn't moved."

"Really?" Marian stood up she was so excited. "You could come with me, Nicholas."

"Sit down, Marian," her mother told her firmly.

"Uh, I'm sorry." I glanced toward Mom for help. "I'm . . . uh, busy painting."

"You don't have to help all day, Nicholas. Maybe you could go later," Mom suggested.

"I don't have my suit. It's still packed somewhere." I tried to signal Mom with my eyes.

"Well, maybe another time then." Dr. James slid out of the seat and stood up. "We have to go now, Marian." She smiled at Mom. "It's been a pleasure. I know we'll be seeing more of each other."

After they left, I slurped at my hot chocolate noisily.

"Are you annoyed with me?"

I kept slurping.

Mom shifted in her chair. "Look, maybe Marian's not your first choice for a friend, but you don't have anyone else right now."

"That's not it at all." I put the hot chocolate down. "All these secrets about our house — everyone knows more than I do."

Mom chewed guiltily at her bottom lip for a moment. "I'm sorry, Nicholas. I thought you'd like it better if you didn't know its history. I know I would."

"Why was it empty so long?"

"The man who owned it, Mr. Hendricks, rented it out for a time. He was one of the lawyers who began the boys' home about ten years ago. I think he always hoped to reopen it. When the last tenants moved out, he finally gave up and put it up for sale."

"Last year?"

"That's right. But I gather the local teenagers used it as a party hangout for a few months before we bought it."

Back at the old neighborhood, the kids I hung around with partied at their own houses. It was only an hour away, a different suburb of the same city, but it was like a foreign country. I downed the last mouthful of hot chocolate.

Mom's mouth tightened into a determined smile. "Time to get back. Ready?"

"Ready as ever," I answered, wiping my mouth with a napkin.

Bright and welcoming, Dad's red and white pickup already sat in the driveway as we rolled up.

"I hope nothing's wrong," Mom said as we walked into the house together. "Hi!" She called out loudly, not knowing where Dad was.

Slap! Slap! The noise came from the kitchen and we followed it there. Six foot three and two hundred pounds, with a green flyswatter in his hand, Dad seemed to be putting his entire weight behind each swat at the wasps.

"Hello," Dad called. "Scared you off, did they?" he asked when I stepped into the kitchen. He stopped swatting at wasps to scratch at one of his thick, heavy sideburns.

"Yup." I shrugged my shoulders. "How come you're home?"

Dad grinned wryly. Black Irish, Mom calls him. I'd always thought it was because of his hair color. Except over the past month, it's greyed over. "Cracked the skylight I was installing this morning. I ordered a replacement but it won't be in until tomorrow." Slap! Another wasp fell to the floor. "Screen's got a hole in it," Dad explained when he noticed me cringing from the wasps. "Was the window open?"

Mom nodded. "Just a hairline."

"Well, with the rain and the time of year, that's all it takes. They're looking for a place to hibernate."

"Where did they all come from?" I asked him.

"There's a wasp colony between the bricks. I'll spray it when they're asleep. They won't bother us anymore."

"Good," Mom and I said at the same time. It was great to have Dad home for a change even if he had to botch a job to manage it. Mom's mood lifted instantly. "I'll put a roast in the oven. We'll have our first family dinner in our new house."

Dad and I painted walls together the rest of the day. Dad whistled over the sound of the roller:

Tchaikovsky, *Dance of the Swans*, Mom's favorite. I couldn't remember him ever whistling like that when he worked at Ford Motors. The smell of fresh paint mixed with the aroma of roast beef, and although it stayed grey and dismal outside, inside it felt peaceful, almost like home. Almost, except for the questions that nagged at me.

"Dad, what was on my wall before you sprayed it?"

"Hmm?" He stopped whistling. "Ah, kid's stuff. Something about 'For a good time call so and so.'" He grinned at me. "Sorry, I forget the actual number."

"That's too bad. I could use a friend." I concentrated on rolling paint for a while. "Do you know anything about the accident that happened at this house?"

"Accident?" Dad repeated.

I frowned at him. Did he really not know or was he playing Mom's game? "Forget it," I told him.

Only, of course, I couldn't. Dr. James had been holding back about our house. Why? And what about the strange dream I'd had last night? *The first dream in a new house always comes true*, Mom had said. I shuddered.

4

Next morning, my brain stuffed with cotton, I stared at the face in the bathroom mirror that looked white and grey from lack of sleep. What was that piece of paper stuck in the corner?

Nicholas, before you do anything today, please mow the lawn. Dad.

Fun, fun.

I took a deep breath and followed the aroma of coffee down to Hell's Kitchen, quickly checking everywhere, the light, the wall. Phew — no buzzing bodies anywhere. I pitched Dad's note in the garbage, fixed myself my usual milky coffee and sipped.

The sun streaming through the kitchen window almost made the yard look inviting. Mug in hand, I slid back the patio door and stepped out. Already the morning felt too warm. Better hurry with that lawn, it was going to be a scorcher, I thought and glanced at the graveyard. The mist rose from the ground as though the graves were steaming.

"Want to come swimming later?" a voice called.

I jumped.

Marian. This was getting to be a habit. She hovered near her back door, watching me — for just how long? I tried not to show my annoyance. "Swimming? Maybe. If I finish painting."

"I'll call on you at one o'clock." The patio door slid shut behind her.

Now something tickled at my hand, and I brushed it away. Another annoyance. No, a wasp! This time I windmilled it away with one arm as I dashed inside, splashing coffee everywhere. The wasp bounced helplessly off the glass as I slammed the patio door shut. I sighed with relief as I leaned against a counter. Another normal day at the Winfield Home.

I fingered the key slot in the banged-up old cupboard door near my head. Mom had the keys but didn't use them. Imagine having to lock up food, imagine having food locked away from you. I shook my head, fixed myself some cereal and dawdled over it as long as I could. Finally, I had to head outside and face the lawn and the insects living in it.

Picking up branches and rocks from the ground, I did the safety thing Dad taught me to always do. Then

I dragged the lawnmower from the garage and started it, guiding it around the edges of the backyard.

Around and around, the drone of the motor put me in some other world so I couldn't tell what I was thinking except that suddenly — crack — the lawnmower hit something. Something rock hard.

The mower shook and rattled uncontrollably. I stopped the engine and tilted the machine. One blade was bent, another had a chunk missing. The lawn now sported a Mohawk.

Dad wouldn't be too thrilled. I knelt down to check the ground. What was it I'd hit? There lay the piece of blade but no stone or anything that had been flung up by the mower. I ran my fingers over the grass and felt something cold and hard. What was it? For a moment, I pictured a pirate treasure chest buried just under the surface of the earth. Marian and her stories.

I probed a little more. It felt like the top of a tombstone. I shuddered and pulled my hand away, aware suddenly of voices shouting in the graveyard.

The Stick Lady and a man who looked to be the caretaker were arguing, Mrs. Dobroski gesturing wildly with her cane.

"Go ahead. No one's going to listen, you crazy old bat." The caretaker shook his head and then shuffled into the stone hut.

That didn't stop the Stick Lady. She continued yelling, the words loud but unclear. She shook her stick in the air some more and then finally moved away, walking toward our fence.

"Good morning, Sasha," she said as she stepped

closer, her accent making her words sound harsh and bitten off.

"Hi," I answered. "My name is Nicholas. I'm not —"

"Of course not. I see that now. Forgive me, Nicholas. My brain is old." Suddenly she raised up her cane in the direction of the caretaker's hut. "But not so old that I don't see what is going on around here."

I didn't know what to say. She calmed down pretty quickly anyway, and turned back to me.

"Please, won't you come to my house some time? I live over there. There are so many things to be done and I am all alone."

"Uh, I'm pretty busy helping my parents right now."

"Yes, you always were a good boy. Very well." Again she pointed with her cane. "When you have time, Sasha, please. The eavestrough needs cleaning."

"Sure," I answered. Humor her, I figured. And then she walked away. I took off too, leaving the tombstone and the lawnmower behind me.

Back inside the house, I washed the sweat from my face and carried the towel with me to the stairs.

"Nicholas?" Mom called from the top of a stepladder. Paint on her nose and cap, she held a roller in her hand. But her hand shook and her smile looked forced. "Sleep well?"

"Great," I lied. "You?"

"No. I kept your dad up, tossing and turning." She shook her head. "I don't know. I had the strangest dreams. Probably just need to get used to the place."

What did you dream? I might have asked in the other house. There it seemed a safe question. But what if Mom

27

had seen that shape in the backyard too? Wouldn't that make it not a dream? And if it wasn't, didn't that make living in this house a very real nightmare?

"The paint fumes don't help either," I told her, hoping she would go on.

But Mom just shrugged and nodded. The circles under her eyes looked darker. Did she know something more? Had she seen something? I opened my mouth to ask, but when she noticed me staring at her, she looked away.

Fine. I took a roller and tray and headed for my own bedroom, determined not to think about it anymore.

After covering the white smears with the second coat of paint, I put on a cheery front for Mom's sake. "It's looking better already," I told her as she stepped into the room.

"Just wait till we take that awful carpet out. There's hardwood floor underneath," she answered enthusiastically.

"Sure, it'll be great." I started whistling. *Dance of the Swans*, what else. Block out all the bad feelings, and we could feel cosy and secure like yesterday. Dad was happy in his new business, there was no going back to the old house anyway. Dreams or not, we were stuck here.

After lunch Marian did drag me off to the pool, chatting at me the whole way. "It's not so scary since you moved in. I can see you painting from my room."

"Oh yeah?" She was watching me. I didn't like that.

"Yeah. I hated staring at those horrible red letters they painted across your wall."

"What did the letters say?" Something in Marian's attitude made me know Dad lied.

Marian bit at her lips.

"C'mon. Everyone else knows but me."

She hesitated for an extra second and then she spoke quickly. "Murderer. And the paint trickled down from the letters so that it looked like blood."

"Who did it?"

"I don't know." Her words tumbled out as though she were hiding something. "Older boys, I think. I never saw them."

"I wonder if it meant something. Do you suppose a murderer slept in my room before?"

"No," Marian answered as though she were slamming a door.

Was she holding back on me like Mom? Nah, she didn't know anything, she didn't understand things. There was no way I was going to discuss what I'd seen in the backyard with her, no matter what I'd agreed to earlier. I decided to forget about everything and enjoy swimming.

We arrived at the pool before it was open to the public.

"They're practicing lifesaving today," Marian explained as we watched a lifeguard drag a dummy out of the pool. "I like to come early to watch. It helps me remember."

"Watch for signs of breathing, Sean!" an older lifeguard instructed. "See if the chest rises. If nothing happens, check the carotid artery for a pulse. Begin compressions only if there are none."

The dummy obviously had no pulse and the junior lifeguard, Sean, started pumping at its chest. "One and two and three and four and five," he called out.

Whoever uses this stuff? I thought, but I watched anyway — especially the great-looking blonde puffing into the dummy's mouth. The blonde brought the dummy to life, and finally the gates opened.

I love pools — the smell, the sounds, even the color of the water, aquamarine like the ocean on a postcard. But as I listened to the laughing and shouting around me, suddenly something gripped my stomach.

That chemical odor. Chlorine. It's what I'd been smelling off and on back at the house. Despite the heat, I shivered, and a warning sign flashed in my brain. Even though chlorine doesn't smell one bit like natural gas, I remembered a card we'd got from the gas company, one that you scratched and sniffed so that you'd recognize the odor if there was ever a leak around your home or neighborhood. Right then, I was feeling as many alarms go off as I would if I'd smelled gas. I stood there in shock, trying to understand what it meant.

Whap! A volleyball smacked against the side of my face and snapped me out of my daze. A whistle shrieked and I saw the blond lifeguard motion to a tall teenager with a shaved head. He'd thrown the ball, I guess.

"You did that on purpose," the lifeguard yelled.

"Did not. It was an accident," the bald kid answered.

"Why do you have to throw it so hard? You could've hurt him."

"You call that hard?"

"Go on over and apologize." The lifeguard dug her fists into her hips.

"Aw, c'mon."

"Apologize or leave, Ryan." Now she glared at him, unblinking.

The bald kid finally nodded in defeat, but as he headed my way he cursed loudly.

His eyes challenged as he came up to me. "I'm sorry, man. You okay?" The two small rings piercing his left eyebrow lifted as he smiled.

I sized the kid up. The expression around his mouth told me he was ready to laugh at me.

I shrugged. "It's not your fault. If I'd been awake, I would've ducked in time."

"All right." He slapped my arm and ran off. The whistle shrieked again. The kid ignored it and climbed up the stairs of the diving board. I noticed another guy almost as bald as he was right behind him, and then a younger boy with more hair.

The guy who'd hit me cannonballed off the board, sending waves of water up over the sides and splashing the angry lifeguard. Before she could dry herself off, the next kid dived with another huge splash that hit her. And then the little boy imitated them. Only he was so little, he didn't know how to swim. The second kid grabbed hold of his arm and pulled him to the side.

The lifeguard marched over to the first guy. She pointed at him and his friend and then angrily thumbed toward the exit.

"Aw, what did we do wrong?" the second kid argued.

"He ran on the deck." She pointed to the bald one.

"Yeah. What about me?"

"You got on the diving board before he was off. Plus neither of you waited to make sure the coast was clear before diving."

"Aw, so what? You're just picking on us."

"That's right. Now get out of here."

He started swearing as he followed the balder one out through the gate.

The little kid grumbled as he tagged after them. "Aw, man! Now I can't stay."

The hairless club hung around the fence talking. Were they waiting till the lifeguard left for the day? I'd be worried if I were her. Or were they waiting for me? They were looking my way. I decided to do a cannonball myself to show that I wasn't some goody two shoes that they should gang up against. It was a big splashy one too, and I got the lifeguard again. "Uh, sorry," I shrugged.

She smiled, took off her sunglasses and rolled incredible green eyes. I liked her instantly. Mom would have said she had too dark a tan for her health, but it set off her streaky blond hair perfectly. And her eyes laughed along with her mouth.

"Uh, Nicholas?" Marian interrupted before I had a chance to introduce myself to the lifeguard.

"What is it?" I snapped. I'd lost the attention of the girl now.

"Those guys want to talk to you." Marian pointed to the fence where the hairless club stood.

Oh great. Depending on how I behaved now, I

could have them bugging me the rest of my life. And they looked like the kind of kids who belonged at the Home. I grabbed my towel first and dried off slowly so as not to appear anxious. Then I ambled over. "Yeah, what's up?"

"Jeff here still wants to swim." The guy who'd whapped me with the volleyball gestured to the young boy with him. "But you have to be seven years old to stay alone."

"Right." I stared back into the challenging eyes, not even daring to blink.

"Leech and I thought maybe you'd babysit for us."

"I'm not a baby, Ryan."

"Yeah, yeah."

Would saying yes be a sign of weakness? I glanced over at the guy called Leech who had his arms folded casually across his chest. I looked down at Jeff. "Please?" he begged, tilting his freckled face to the side. His eyes looked as though they were expecting a no.

He made me remember all the hot summer days of my life when there was no one to take me to the pool. Aw, what the heck. "No problem," I answered Ryan.

"Good. She can tell you where we live." Ryan gestured with his head toward Marian. "So, catch you around, eh?"

"Sure," I answered. But Leech and Ryan were already off, laughing and jostling one another.

Jeff ran through the entrance and jumped into the water at the shallow end. I decided to do another dive and maybe catch the lifeguard's eye again. I stood at the end of the diving board for a few seconds, bounced a couple of times and did a slow head-first. When I broke through the surface again, I noticed I had all the lifeguard's attention and smiled. She dove in, but swam right past me. I watched her as she grabbed Jeff's arm.

"I told you not to dive until you know how to swim!" she hollered as she helped him to the ladder.

"Aw, I would have made it," Jeff grumbled as he climbed up.

The lifeguard followed behind him. "Never mind," she said when she stood on the deck beside Jeff. "One more time and you're out with your brother. Who's looking after you, anyway?"

"Hi." I swam up to the ladder. "I'm Nicholas. I'm supposed to be taking care of, uh, Jeff. I'm sorry, I just didn't expect him to dive in."

"Well, okay, Nicholas. I'm holding you responsible for what he does." Her forehead crinkled and she sounded serious, but then she smiled, a perfect white-toothed smile.

In that moment, I felt as though moving might have been worthwhile after all.

"Okay." I smiled back. When she walked away, I turned to Jeff. "What did you do that for? Are you crazy? You could've drowned."

"Nah. That's how my dad learned to swim. Someone just threw him into the deep end."

"So you're throwing yourself in?"

"Yup." Jeff grinned at me.

"Why don't you take lessons?"

"I just told you why. Because it's the way Dad

learned and he said it was good enough for me."

"Well, don't jump when I'm supposed to be watching you or I'll take you home."

With no brothers and sisters of my own, I didn't know what to do with Jeff so I was glad when Marian took over. Actually it was like she'd found the perfect playmate. They played shark and threw each other off an inner tube. I joined in for a while but mostly I just watched the lifeguard with the great smile.

When it was time to go, Marian took Jeff's hand and Jeff took mine. That sure felt strange. We dropped him off at a house on the other side of the graveyard. In the window, standing with his hands on his hips, I saw the caretaker who'd been arguing with Mrs. Dobroski earlier.

"That's my dad!" Jeff broke away from us. "I gotta go. Thanks!"

Marian shuddered.

"What's wrong with you?" I asked as we started walking away.

"Mr. McNamara." Marian frowned. "My mother says to always stay away from him."

"Why?"

"Because." Marian looked uncomfortable.

"That's no answer."

"Jeff came to see Mom once with a broken arm."

"McNamara did that to him?"

"We're not sure. My mother says Jeff may just be accident prone. He's hy . . . hyper . . ." Marian paused, frowning.

"Hyperactive?" I finished for her.

"Nicholas, my mother —" Marian's face crumpled as though Dr. James was there and had just criticized her. "I'm not supposed to talk about Mom's patients. Please don't tell anyone," she begged.

"Poor kid. Where's his mother when all this is happening?"

"She left them a long time ago. I don't know if Jeff ever sees her."

I looked back toward Jeff's house. The yard looked about as well cared for as ours. "I guess there's nothing we can do," I sighed. "Come on. Let's cut through the graveyard. It's faster."

We didn't stop to read any tombstones this time because I spotted my father through our fence, standing over the broken lawnmower in the middle of the backyard where I'd left it.

5

"Dad, I swear, I checked the whole lawn and didn't miss a single branch or stone."

"I believe you." Dad surveyed the damaged lawn-mower blade. "What could you have possibly hit?"

"A tombstone. Here, see?" I brushed back the grass with my fingers.

Dad knelt down and ran his fingers over the hard ridge poking out of the earth. "Tombstone! Hah! You and your mother have some imagination."

What did she imagine? I wondered. I stared at Dad for some hint but he was concentrating on the ridge in front of him. "I don't know what it is, a concrete wall, maybe. But it's definitely not a tombstone."

"Good. So no one's buried here?"

Dad shook his head. "Around the part you hit, the earth's shifted and sunken more. The rest of the wall's still buried."

"Why would anyone build a concrete wall in the middle of the yard and then bury it?"

"Who knows? But you and I have other things to worry about right now. Like getting a new blade. There's still time to finish mowing this lawn before dark."

At the local Build-all, the right size blade for our mower cost a lot more than Dad expected.

He looked into his wallet and frowned.

"I'm sorry, Dad."

He waved his hand. "It's what credit cards are for." He pulled out his Build-all card. "They let me exchange the cracked skylight this morning, anyway. That would have cost me a lot more than replacing this blade."

"Dad, what do you mean about Mom having a lot of imagination too? Did she mention seeing anything?"

"Your mom says our new house is unhappy. Not at peace, you know? Which reminds me, let's have a look at the kitchen displays."

We wandered over to the rows of cupboards.

"I'd like to replace all those beatup cupboard doors, get rid of the stupid locks. Hey, this would be a great idea too." Dad touched a towel bar that ran the length of one of the display counters. "She could do her stretches with this!" He smiled and took some figures down in his notepad. "I'll order these doors and the bar. It'll be a surprise for her."

When we returned to the house, he and I carefully

paced the yard checking for other strange obstacles.

"What'll we do about that ridge?" I asked Dad.

"We should probably raise the ground with another layer of topsoil. For now, just clip it by hand along the rock."

About an hour later, I finished the back and front lawn without hitting anything else. The grass in the back looked trampled down and unhealthy, plus now it had a tooth sticking out of the middle. Dad was right, it would probably be better to bury the whole yard and start all over. And maybe bulldoze the house down while we were at it.

I had an uneasy feeling even that wouldn't help. That a new split level built on the same property would still have a ghost floating in the backyard. That the word MURDERER would somehow reappear in bloody letters on a new bedroom wall, that wasps would still swarm. That sleep here would always be filled with nightmares.

Lying on my mattress that night, I wondered about the strange wall buried in the grass. Was it part of a jail cell? Did everything about this place have to be abnormal? I took a deep breath, ready to let it out in a sigh when I realized the smell was back. Chlorine. I recognized it now. I felt the pain again too — the powerful wrenching at my stomach, the longing. It was a pain that somehow did not belong to me, as if perhaps I was feeling someone else's sorrow. But whose? I rushed to the window and saw it again.

Quietly, I snuck down the stairs into the kitchen and from the patio window, the glowing shape stood close enough to make out human details. A boy's face, my age. He moved slowly through the fence, coming closer and closer. At the strange tooth poking through our back lawn, he stopped. We watched each other. Then he moved down and down again, sinking into the earth. He seemed to be looking for something. Whatever it was, he couldn't find it and climbed out again. Confused, disorientated, woozy, I felt I could almost understand what he was thinking, if I would only concentrate more.

I slid back the patio door and the figure sensed my presence, stopping and turning to face me.

I walked toward him. The odor of chlorine became stronger and stronger. It burned at my nostrils. My eyes watered and my throat tightened. I wanted to gag. I needed to back away. The boy continued to face me, intently watching.

"What is it that you want?" I called out in a voice that didn't sound like my own. Pain and longing made the words crack. The figure rested for another heart-beat, then turned away, as though disappointed. I stared after it as it slipped back into the graveyard, and continued staring until well after it dissolved into the night air.

"You're up late. Feeling all right?" Mom greeted me when I staggered into the kitchen the next morning.

"Yeah. Just having trouble sleeping." I grabbed a bran muffin from the plate in the middle of the table and bit into it. "Mom, it's too quiet in here. How come there's no music on?"

"We haven't connected the stereo yet."

"Oh! I'm going to do that right now." I headed for the family room, desperate to bring life into this house.

"Nicholas, why don't you finish your breakfast first?"

I was already connecting, right speaker wire into the red hole, left into the white. I fiddled with all the plugs and wires for about fifteen minutes. Then I set up the speakers at opposite ends of the room and turned on a rock station. I expected Mom to say something. "Could you turn that down?" or "Could you switch the station?"

Instead she toyed with her coffee spoon while I polished off a couple muffins and a glass of milk. "C'mon, Nicholas, one more coat and the walls upstairs will look perfect," she finally said.

Section by section, room by room, rolling the paint on frantically, Mom and I covered up the walls and their secrets, while between us another wall grew. Whitewashing unhappiness didn't seem to work. At noon we stood back to admire our efforts.

Mom frowned.

"It looks wonderful, Mom. Honest. No more coats, please?"

Mom eyed the walls and then the floor. She pursed her lips, then looked at me. "We've got to rip up that carpet. I want to see the wood underneath."

I felt ready to fall into bed. "Sure, Mom."

More heavy, hot work, the only thing Mom would

share with me. Beneath the carpet, row by row, the oak strips appeared, a film of dust and lint still hiding their condition. At one end, I needed to lift the heating vent.

"Hey, look what I found." From inside the vent, I picked up a paper, yellow and brittle with age.

"What is it?" Mom asked.

"Some kid's picture. See?" I held it out to her. Drawn in thick wax crayon, two stick people with baseball-mitt hands seemed to be playing in a pool, one going down a slide, the other diving off a board. Scrawled in big sloppy letters at the bottom were two names: Corey and Sasha. They rang a bell somehow but not loud enough for me to make a real connection.

"Nicholas, could you daydream later? We're almost finished."

"All right." I put the drawing on top of one of the boxes in the hall and continued rolling up the carpet with Mom. Hauling the rug down the stairs and out the door was an even dirtier, clumsier job. We flopped down exhausted on the couch in the family room after propping the roll of carpet against the side of the house.

Before my breathing even returned to normal, Mom leapt up again, grabbing a bucket and mop.

"What are you trying to prove?" I called after her.

"I have to clean that floor. I want to have one perfect room right now so we'll have a vision of what the house can be. For all of us," she added.

"Fine, wash floors in the temple of gloom," I mumbled, shaking my head. "I need some R and R." I grabbed my suit and a towel from the ground floor bathroom. "I'm off to the pool," I called out louder.

"Are you calling on Marian?"

I pretended not to hear. I wanted the chance to make new friends, but didn't want to explain that to Mom. "Bye," I called back and dashed out of the house. I kept on running, out of the yard and down the street, hoping Marian wouldn't see me.

The pool wasn't open when I arrived. A line of younger kids stood in front of the gate and a gang of kids my age hung around the park alongside of the pool. No lifesaving lessons today.

For a second, I felt out of place. I wished I was six or seven and could just walk up to someone and say, "Hey, wanna play?" and just as easy as that I would have a new friend.

I watched the older kids for a while. They were in a kind of circle, laughing, jostling each other. I wanted so badly to be laughing easily alongside them, no ghosts on my mind. There were a few girls, long legs, long hair, straight white smiles. I stared at a brunette who had a tattoo of a rose on her shoulder. She caught me staring and whispered to someone in the center of the circle.

"Hey, Nicholas. C'mon over!" It was a friendly voice. Ryan stepped out of the circle and waved me over. The tattooed girl had been whispering to him.

I felt a rush of relief at knowing someone, anyone, but it looked as though Ryan was an especially good person to know at this moment. I'd made the right decision yesterday, taking care of Jeff.

When I got to the group, I noticed Leech standing

beside him. "Hi. Where's Jeff?" I asked Ryan.

"Don't look now, he's standing in line with your girlfriend," Leech answered.

Already it was happening. I glanced back over to the group of younger kids and there she was. Marian. Unfortunately, she spotted me at that moment too, and grinned.

"She's not my girlfriend," I told him, too hotly.

Marian was waving wildly now. "Hi, Nicholas!" Her happy voice and big smile made me seem like a liar. I tried not to look over.

Ryan laughed and I knew at that moment, I had a choice to make. I could wave back and join her and forever after be ignored, or worse, by this group of kids. Or I could do something I would never have done before. Which was to turn my back on her, pretending I hadn't heard or seen her.

Ryan laughed again and this time I joined him.

6

Ryan and his friends spat on the ground and swore loudly as they walked into the pool area. You could see the lifeguards giving each other uneasy looks. If I were back in my old neighborhood, I wouldn't have been caught dead with them. But here I was alone. I felt my step turn into a swagger, my voice grow louder.

Rose, the girl with the tattoo, snapped her towel at me in a challenge, a full-lipped smile on her creamy-skinned face. I swore at her, something else I never do.

The pale green eyes of the lifeguard looked over, her sunglasses in my direction. Her mouth opened and then closed again. Her eyes narrowed and she shook her head.

"Hey, you're turning all red, Nick." Trust Leech to

call me by the short form I hated. "What's the matter? You got the hots for Shannon?"

"I don't even know any Shannon."

"The Goddess," Leech hitched his thumb in the lifeguard's direction. "C'mon, you don't fool me." Leech made smacking kiss noises while giving me calf-eyes.

"Ah, leave him alone," Ryan told Leech.

Leech ignored Ryan and continued. "Oh yeah, I forgot, Nicky loves Marian." More kiss noises. Hardy har har. Leech and the girls thought he was pretty funny. I couldn't let him get away with it.

"That's right." I casually put my arm around Rose's waist to bug Leech. His eyes sent Keep Off messages to me. "All the girls. Marian and Shannon and Rose, here."

Leech knocked my arm away. "Leave her alone."

"Sure. But can Rose leave me alone?" Her hand rested on my shoulder and I stroked her cheek with my fingers.

She broke away, laughing. Rose patted the stubble on Leech's head, teasing him and Ryan about their lack of hair. Ryan and Leech dragged her toward the pool.

"You wouldn't!" Rose called loudly. "Don't you dare." She struggled and screamed all the way. By the time they reached the pool's edge, everyone there had to be watching.

"No, don't!" she hollered.

It was the last bit of encouragement Ryan and Leech needed. One good shove and she was in.

Shannon blew her whistle sharply and then marched over. She didn't yell, but her voice seemed controlled as though she wanted to. She pointed to the sign and read directly from it: "No pushing, shoving or horseplay." Then added, "Last warning."

Leech and Ryan snickered and swore the moment Shannon walked away.

I desperately wanted those pale green eyes to look my way again. So as soon as Rose came back to us, dripping and laughing, I caught her up in my arms, ran over to the pool and dumped her in again. Shannon couldn't just ignore me.

I glanced back to see her reaction and saw her shake her head again, and frown.

The whistle shrieked. Shannon motioned over another lifeguard, Sean, her lifesaving partner from the practice. The two of them came at us, shoulder to shoulder. "Time to go, guys," Sean suggested. He folded arms that were heavy with muscle across his wide chest.

"Why us? He threw her in," Leech argued, pointing at me. "Shannon only told us about that rule a minute ago."

"That's too bad. Maybe tomorrow you'll read the rules all by yourself." He grabbed my elbow and pulled me toward the changing room.

"Nicholas?" I heard the shock in Marian's voice and ignored her. Maybe now she'd stop hovering and watching.

"I wanna leave with my brother." Jeff broke away from Marian and ran toward us. Leech and I stood on either side of Ryan. Jeff hesitated, then chose to walk beside me. We took our time putting on our clothes to bug Muscle Guard Sean, after which he walked us through the gate.

Rose and the other girls smiled and giggled at us from behind the pool fence, but they stayed behind. They weren't going to miss their swim. I kept my head high, walking tall and slow in case Shannon was watching, but when I turned I saw her chatting with Sean. For one moment my eyes caught hers. She didn't look impressed. Then she threw back her head and laughed hard.

Jeff still walked alongside me, every once in a while looking up at me and grinning. His eyes shone and he tried to match his footsteps to mine.

"Let's go to the arcade," Leech suggested.

"Yeah! I wanna play Space Invaders," Jeff chimed in.

"Oh yeah?" Leech sneered at Jeff. "Got any money, kid?"

Jeff reached deep into his pockets and his mouth turned downward.

"Maybe Nick will share his with you," Leech suggested in a smug tone, as though he knew no one in their right mind would ever give the kid a chance at the video games.

"Sure, I've got some change he can have," I said, mostly to get Leech's goat. I rooted out all the coins from my pockets and handed them to him.

Jeff's mouth turned back up in a toothy grin that took up his whole face. "Thanks, Nicholas, thanks a lot." He fingered the coins, counting them. There was at least a couple of dollars.

"Yeah." Leech rolled his eyes. "You're a regular saint, Nick. Heh heh, get it? Saint Nick."

"Can we just go?" Ryan broke in impatiently.

"Where is this arcade?" I asked. I wasn't even sure I was supposed to come along but I didn't want to go home early and have to explain why.

"At the mall. We could take the bus." Ryan reached into his pocket the same way that his kid brother had a minute ago. "Nah. Let's walk. It's not so far."

"We need some cash. What's up with your old man, anyway?" Leech asked.

"Shut up," Ryan answered. He shifted his eyes in my direction.

And big, tough Leech did as he was told. I pretended not to notice anything. What was the big deal? Did they do gravedigging for Ryan's dad or something? I wondered as we started walking.

The mall was far. Too far in the hot, mid-afternoon sun. We passed the Power House area, mansions with interlock driveways and color-coordinated shrubbery that reminded me of my old neighborhood.

Leech eyed the houses with a tight grin on his face. What was he doing, casing them? When he caught me watching, he smiled even harder, cracking his knuckles.

Five or ten blocks later, there were bungalows again, then row houses and finally apartment buildings. We passed a hospital, St. Luke's, and from that point on the street was lined with offices and stores.

We stopped in front of an antique shop. FAIR-CHILD'S TREASURES the letters across the window read. A scruffy, worn-out bear sat under a Tiffany lamp on display.

"A hundred bucks for a wrecked bear! We could pick stuff like that up at a garage sale for a quarter," Leech commented. "Your old man should pay us more."

"Shut up, will ya?" Ryan made eye signals toward me, and again, Leech just took it.

It didn't sound like he was talking about garage sale browsing. Or gravedigging for that matter. Kids I knew in the old neighborhood shoplifted occasionally. CDs, small stuff, not something I'd ever do, but then again, not something I'd squeal about either. I made myself ignore them again.

We continued walking another couple of blocks to the mall. When we cut through the parking lot, I spotted a big C curled around an R, the Crown Realty logo. I'd gone there with Mom when she signed the final offer. Now I remembered what Mom had said the first day in the house. There'd been an accident years ago. Mom didn't want to know any more details but that didn't stop me from asking. We pushed through the mall doors and the artificially cold air hit us immediately.

"I'll join you later," I told the hairless club. "I'm going to drop by the real estate office."

"Gonna buy another house, St. Nick?" Leech jeered. "Good. We want our party room back."

"What'd you say?" I didn't understand what he meant.

"Never mind," Ryan told me. "We'll see you."

"See you," Jeff repeated as he ran after his brother.

I turned toward the mall map mounted behind some Plexiglas in the corner and figured out which way to go from the You Are Here arrow. Then I walked. Beside the Telephone Boutique, I noticed pictures of houses on the window and recognized the Crown Realty office.

"I'm looking for a real estate agent," I told the grey-haired man sitting at the front desk. "I can't remember her name. She had this laugh, um . . ."

"Sort of like Goofy?" The agent played with his glasses.

I nodded.

"That would be my partner, Ellen Drake." He glanced back at the list on the wall and we both saw the large red button under the OUT sign at the same time.

"She's not here right now, but maybe I could help you in some way?"

"I wonder if you could give me some information about the house she sold my parents. It's on Winfield Drive. Over by the graveyard."

"I'm sorry. I wasn't her partner when she got that listing. I'm sure your parents could call her later for whatever they want to know."

Call back later, an I-can't-be-bothered kind of brushoff. I tried something different. "One thing my mom wanted was a picture of the house. We're doing a lot of work on it and she wanted something to remind her of what it looked like before." It wasn't a lie and I thought I'd get to see what our house looked like when it was the Home.

"Didn't she get that with the features sheet?"

"No. We didn't get one with a picture."

"Oh. That's odd. They always come with a picture unless the house is a total wreck." He still didn't seem anxious to help me.

I gave him a little push. "My friend's family is thinking of selling. I was telling her about Crown Realty. Could you check Ms. Drake's file maybe?"

"Sure. Here's my card. Frank Sheffield." He reached over and shook my hand. "Why don't you step into my office in the back here?"

I followed him and he took out a file from the cabinet behind him. "No, no picture. That's odd. Hold on. What's this doing in here? Hmm." He took a photograph out of the folder. "Your house doesn't have an in-ground pool, does it?" he asked.

"No. May I see that anyway?"

Sheffield passed me the snapshot and I recognized the back of our house, the blood-stain colored brick, the two patio windows, kitchen and family room. But there were a couple of happy-looking people too old to be young offenders sitting under a patio umbrella. What was even more surprising, as Sheffield had said, there was an in-ground pool, a large one with a diving board on the short side nearest the graveyard, and a slide on the long side away from Marian's house; and of course the water, in the middle, all turquoise and peaceful. It made me want to jump into the picture.

"At least what I meant was, not anymore. Our house doesn't have an in-ground pool." I didn't hand the photograph back to Sheffield and he looked uncomfortable suddenly. I slid the photo into my back pocket.

"Do you mind giving me your name and phone number?" he asked, his brow furrowed. "Maybe when Ellen gets back, she can give you a call."

"Sure." I jotted it down for him. "Thank you very much, Mr. Sheffield. I'll pass your card on."

He nodded.

"Is the arcade this way?" I asked as I went out the door.

"Just past the food court, hang a left, you can't miss it."

"Thanks again," I told him and then bumped into the hairless club before I'd taken five steps. That is, they bumped into me. Hard. Jostling me and laughing. My hands curled into fists before I realized it was them. A security guard standing in front of a water fountain stared at us openly.

"Do you have any extra money?" Ryan asked me.

"The Virtual Death game just came in!" Jeff explained breathlessly.

"Only five bucks," I said, hoping that would throw him off.

"Great!" Ryan reached out his hand and I stuffed a crumpled bill into it. "Just till Friday. I got some money coming to me then."

Back at the arcade with no money left, Jeff and I could only watch as an attendant harnessed Ryan and Leech in separate black pods, facing each other. Virtual Death was one of those high-tech "five minutes for five dollars" games. High action, low skill with some co-operation.

Ryan and Leech became skeletons hunting a beast

on a little screen mounted on the ceiling. Their loud curses and insults were broadcast over the entire arcade by sound systems in their helmets. No cooperation, lots of temper.

By the time their skeletons disintegrated and they were transformed into eternal slaves of the beast, Ryan was shaking his head and swearing at Leech. "You never listen to anyone, do you?" He shoved him hard and Leech staggered, grabbing hold of the side of the pod.

All that, over a stupid game.

Surprisingly, Leech didn't answer back.

"Aw, let's go home now. I'm not in the mood to hang around," Ryan finally said, his face red with anger.

Best idea I'd heard all day.

Leech still had nothing to say. He just kept his head down and followed us out, quietly.

The walk home seemed way longer than the walk there. "Can't we take the bus home?" Jeff whined as he dragged his feet.

"No, we can't. We used up all our money," Ryan snapped.

"Why do we have to wait for your old man to set us up anyway?" Leech found his mouth again.

"Why don't you ever shut up!"

Leech stopped then, deliberately turning my way, his mouth stretching into a skinny-eyed smile. He hadn't forgotten me, he had spoken out because of me.

We walked for a long time without anyone saying anything until we reached Mrs. Dobroski's bungalow.

"The Stick Lady's house!" Jeff ducked over to my other side to be farther away from her home.

"That's right," Leech commented. "Did you get a load of all the jewelry she wears? Bet Fairchild would like that stuff."

"Probably fake."

"Nah, she comes from the old country. Those people always have tons of gold."

"I don't care. She gives my father a hard time as it is."

"So we could give her a hard time back."

"Leave it alone, will ya, Leech."

"My turn-off here. So long, guys," I said as I took off along the shortcut through the graveyard. As desperate as I was for friends, I made a promise to myself to steer clear of the hairless club. They were trouble, plain and simple.

"So long, Saint Nick," Leech yelled.

"See you tomorrow, Nicholas," Jeff called. The hope in his voice tugged at me. There was a kid as lonely as I was.

I smiled and waved. Only the branches on the trees waved back. The three of them had already taken off.

All the faces of the tombstones watched me and I moved more quickly. I noticed the Stick Lady kneeling in front of her husband's grave, her lips moving. I hurried by her, feeling guilty about what Leech seemed to be planning. Finally, at the fence between my backyard and the cemetery, I climbed over.

Back at the Winfield Home at last! Through the patio window, I could see my parents already sitting down to supper. Loud rock music spilled out into the yard, same station I'd tuned in on that morning. Weird. "Sorry I'm late," I said as I stepped inside.

"No problem. Your chicken's in the microwave," Mom answered.

"Why don't you take a look at your room before you eat? We've moved all your furniture in . . . I think you'll be surprised." Dad winked at me as he chewed a mouthful of chicken.

"Oh yeah?" I climbed the stairs, hot, tired and thirsty. Inside my room, all I saw were white walls, blank windows, and now a glossy wooden floor. It reminded me of something. A library? Or museum maybe? An institution, anyway. And then it hit me — it looked like a room in a home for young offenders. I wasn't surprised at all.

7

Even three coats of bone white paint couldn't brighten the Winfield Home once the sun sank. The posters rolled up in my boxes got unrolled and tried on different walls. But nothing looked right. The trophies got lifted from the box and then just put down again. Somehow nothing fit. So I gave up and undressed for bed. What was that? I felt something in my back pocket.

The photograph. I'd almost forgotten. I pulled the picture out and stared at that inviting water for a long time. In my mind, I saw the ghost slipping down into the earth. He must have been using the stairs, I suddenly thought. That was it, the ghost was using the pool stairs!

I threw my jeans back on, rushed down to the

kitchen and out the patio door. Grabbing a shovel from the shed, I dug near the broken tooth in the lawn. The nighttime quiet made the first clink sound loud enough to wake the dead. Suddenly, a heavy hand grabbed my shoulder. I gasped.

"What the heck are you doing outside at this hour?" Dad asked as he yawned and scratched at his head.

"I wanted to see something." *There's a treasure buried in your backyard*, Marian had told me.

"Why can't it wait for tomorrow? Your mother thought you were some kind of . . ."

Ghost, is what he didn't say. I stabbed the edge of my shovel into the earth and turned to him. The kitchen light shot a wide beam through the patio door, bathing him in a pale yellow glow. I could see a few frazzled grey hairs springing out from his sideburns and even his eyebrows. I noticed the downward tug on the skin of his cheeks as well as underneath his neck. He looked exhausted. What had I looked like to Mom?

"I just needed to know something right away."

"What?" Dad asked as the shovel clinked again.

We both bent down and I brushed away some dirt. Concrete. "It's a step, Dad. A step to the swimming pool buried in our backyard." I handed him the photograph. "Look at this picture, Dad. I got it from Crown Realty."

"Your mom see this?"

"Not yet."

"Too bad it's buried. Wouldn't you have loved your own pool?" Dad shook his head.

"Yes, but . . ." I hesitated. *There's a ghost that haunts*

it. That would have sounded too crazy. I tried to work up to it in a different way. "Do you ever look outside at night and see anything?"

"I can't even read the paper without falling asleep. My head hits the pillow and I'm out," Dad answered.

"Do you ever smell anything?"

"Sure, paint, turpentine, soap. I can't wait till we're finished getting the house set up."

"No. I mean chlorine. Like in a pool."

Dad looked at me. The pupils in his eyes were huge. "Now, that wouldn't be possible, Nicholas. Even if the pool had been buried yesterday." He put his large hand on my shoulder. "C'mon, son. It's time for bed."

He was right. None of it was possible, I thought as I climbed the stairs and headed for my room again.

Mom and Dad had placed my bureau against the wall beneath my window and as I was about to lay the photograph down I noticed the crayon drawing I'd found in the heating vent. I held it up. It was the same pool, the diving board at the back, the slide on the right side and the stairs where I'd seen the ghost descending. The boys in the water could have been Jeff and me but of course they weren't. *Corey and Sasha,* the childish scrawl at the bottom read. Just who were they? I laid both pictures down and got ready for bed.

As ugly and institutional as this whole house looked, I could almost shut it out when I closed my eyes, I was so exhausted. I lay down and fell asleep instantly.

But then I dreamt. I stood on a diving board bouncing gently above the same aquamarine water that was in the photograph. I reached up for the sky and leapt into the air, turning perfectly around into a jackknife dive. When I cut through the surface, I felt the water rushing at me, cool and exhilarating. With long powerful strokes, I swam through it, heading toward the ladder at the side.

Suddenly pain made my stomach clench and I realized something was wrong. What? What? An awareness grew from that pain. Someone was missing and I needed to find him. I searched the bottom of the pool. I swam around in circles, the chlorine stinging my eyes and burning at the back of my throat. But it was no use, I couldn't find him.

Finally, I headed for the surface, an overwhelming heaviness settling onto my arms and legs, anchoring me down. I was almost there now; I just needed to break through and breathe. At the point when my head should have pushed through into the air, it hit something solid. A glass wall. Water filled my mouth and nose, and my lungs were bursting. Again and again, I tried to smash the wall, but I no longer had the energy, and at last I flattened my face against the glass, desperate for air.

As I sank back down, strange laughter echoed through the water. Cartoon laughter, like Goofy. Then I saw faces peering at me through that glass wall: Leech, Ryan, Marian, Dr. James, the Stick Lady and Ellen Drake, the real estate agent. Lots of laughter. Ms. Drake's laughter. I gasped, choked and then I heard the words screaming in my brain. They weren't "Help me!" as I would've expected. I was screaming, "Tell me!"

The sun streamed through my window and I woke up with my mouth hanging open. I sucked back some deep breaths of the hot, humid air. My heart pounded hard at my chest and I felt wet and clammy. Only a dream, I told myself, but somehow I couldn't believe it.

I glanced at my watch. Noon already. So I grabbed a quick shower to rinse off the faint odor of chlorine I could still smell.

Then I was ready to face the day. The house was always easier to take with the sun shining. I threw on some cutoffs and a T-shirt and headed down the stairs. Mom sat outside on the patio, sipping a coffee, looking over toward the graveyard. I saw only her back and shoulders, but she seemed relaxed.

"Hi," I called to her.

She jumped. "Oh, Nicholas, it's you."

"Yeah. Is it safe to come out or are we under wasp attack?"

"It's fine."

I carried out my own milky coffee and a bowl of cereal. Birds twittered and chirped, peaceful and pleasant. I sat down next to Mom and saw what she was looking at. Near a large mound of earth on the side of the cemetery close to Mrs. Dobroski's house, Mr. McNamara leaned against a shovel, wiping his brow with a white handkerchief.

"Mom, have you seen this?" I dropped the photograph on the table in front of her.

"Um, yes. Your father told me you dug up the stairs yesterday." Mom's cheeks colored a bit.

"Another secret you were keeping from me?"

"Well, no. Believe it or not, I really did forget."

Before we moved here, I could always believe her. I squinted at Mom and then back at the graveyard. "Oh my gosh." I pointed to McNamara, as I realized what he was doing. "He's digging a grave."

Mom shrugged her shoulders.

"Ohhh!" I felt a rock sink to the bottom of my stomach. Just a hole, just a hole, I told myself. Still, this hole was for a body and for that reason I couldn't turn away. I swallowed the last of my coffee hard. "Mom, the painting's done. Could you maybe drive me to the old neighborhood?"

She shook her head. "Sorry. No time. I want to enter all your father's new accounts on the computer. Besides, you need to get adjusted to your new home."

Perfect, I thought. Then I heard Marian's voice haunting me from over the fence. Even more perfect.

"Guess what, Mrs. Dilon?"

"What, dear?"

"I passed my lifesaving course. Yesterday I had to rescue a dummy from the water and give him the breath of life."

"Did you save him?" I asked.

"Sort of. Only, well . . . Mom told me lots of times you can make people breathe again, but their brains are pretty much dead, so they die later on."

"That's nice, Marian." Mom smiled, ignoring the more gruesome details. "You must be proud."

"Now I can be a lifeguard." She grinned for a moment and then the edges of her mouth turned down. "Probably no one will hire me, but I could still save someone if I had to." She stopped chatting and watched uneasily as Mr. McNamara put his equipment away. "Call on you at one for the pool, Nicholas?" she asked after a few moments.

Mom watched me twist my mouth around. Could I even show my face at the pool? Shannon the goddess, the one person who could make this move worthwhile, would be there. "Okay," I finally said and Marian disappeared back into the house.

"That's in five minutes," Mom said, looking at her watch. "Help me clear the dishes away so I can get to work."

"Sure." Mom and I carried our plates inside. She rinsed and I stacked them in the dishwasher. "There's this girl," I started to tell her.

"You're making new friends, that's great."

I opened my mouth to tell her more about Shannon, to ask her advice about catching her attention. At the old house, we talked like this all the time.

"You finish up. I want to get to my office."

"Okay," I answered to no one at all, Mom had dashed off so quickly. I dumped in the dishwasher detergent, and latched the door. As I twisted the dial, I heard the doorbell ring. And ring and ring.

Mom came out of her office looking annoyed. "Come in!" she called exasperated. "Come in, come in, come in," she yelled as the doorbell rang for the sixth time. "Would you just get it, Nicholas!"

Before I could reach the door, it opened and

Marian's straggly haired head poked in. "I'm sorry, I'm a little early, Mrs. Dilon," she said, looking up to where my mother stood on the stair landing.

Mom smiled tightly. "That's all right, Marian. Call me Joanne."

"Oh . . . I . . . my mother would never let me do that!" Marian's eyebrows bunched together.

"C'mon then, let's go," I told her, rushing her out the door to give Mom peace.

We used the cemetery shortcut and, as we passed the headstone with the lamb on it, I slowed to pay an extra bit of attention to it.

Corey Fairchild

That name! Why did it ring bells in my head? Marian didn't even glance back as she rushed ahead of me.

"Marian!" I called as I ran to catch up. "Did Corey Fairchild live in my house before?"

"No. He didn't." Marian, who usually acted like a puppy begging for love, seemed to snap shut like a book.

I saw the crayon drawing in my mind, the stick figures in the pool, the names Corey and Sasha scrawled at the bottom. I saw Marian's back and shoulders rigid and tense ahead of me and at that moment I knew that the Corey buried in that grave must be the same one who had drawn that picture.

I decided not to push it. At least not with Marian. Right then I heard yelling coming from the other side of the gate. Screaming and then crying.

"That's Jeff." Marian covered her mouth as she stared toward the McNamara house.

"Come on," I told her. "We can't just stand here."

Marian shook her head. "My mother said to stay away from McNamara."

"Well, she's not around right now, is she?" I started running through the graveyard gates toward his house. *What could I do, what would I say?* I was pounding on Jeff's door now.

"I'm not buying any." The door flung back and Mr. McNamara stood there. "What d'ya want?" A short man with cement-colored eyes, he wore mud brown work pants and a matching shirt with dirt smudges all over it. Would he beat up on a little kid?

The question burned at me, making me hesitate for another moment. Then I stared straight into his eyes and spoke up. "We were wondering if Jeff wanted to come to the pool with us." We, that was a laugh, Marian still stood at the graveyard gate.

"Jeff!" McNamara turned from me, scratching a bald spot on the back of his freckled head. "Jeff, you get here double quick." His commanding tone and red face reminded me of someone. Yes, I could see where Ryan got his temper.

Jeff appeared from behind his father. He was sniffing and his eyes and nose were red. McNamara shuffled away, grumbling. Running his hand under his nose, Jeff smiled when he saw his father was gone.

"You wanna come swimming with us?" I asked him.

"Yeah." He stepped out quickly and shut the door behind him.

"What about your swimming suit?"

"I always wear one. Just in case." Jeff unzipped his jeans to show me.

"It's all right, Jeff, I believe you."

"What about a towel?" Marian asked when she finally joined us.

Jeff shrugged.

"That's okay. You can use this one," I told him and wrapped my towel around his neck.

Jeff slipped his hand in mine, a move that again surprised me. When he was around his big brother, Jeff acted older and tougher. His small trusting hand reminded me now that he was just a little kid. After all, for a five year old, holding hands wasn't so strange.

"I need your help with something." I squeezed Jeff's hand as we continued walking.

"What?" Jeff asked.

"You too, Marian." With none of Mom's usual "Just be yourself" advice, I had to make my own plan, one that would make Marian give me some breathing room without hurting her feelings.

"Okay, sure," she said trustingly.

"I want to get to know the lifeguard," I told them.

"Shannon?" Jeff asked.

"Yeah. Could you maybe help me?" Did Marian look hurt?

"I know Shannon from my lifesaver's course," Marian answered me. "She's nice." Marian smiled and I was grateful. She was really okay — pretty even, in a childlike way — just as long as she gave me some space.

We separated at the changing rooms and then met

again on the pool deck. I shielded my eyes against the bright sun as I searched the lifeguard chairs for Shannon.

"There she is." Jeff pointed.

"Stop that. Let's not be so obvious. I'm going to do a couple of my best dives and then afterward, I'll walk her way. Maybe you could say something to her about me, okay?"

"What can I do?" Marian asked. She sounded about Jeff's age then.

"You know her. What does she like?"

"Um. I've seen her rollerblading at Skeeters Arena."

"Great, that's a help already. Here I go. Wish me luck." I strode over to the diving board ladder and climbed it, gripping the rail tightly to try and make more muscles show. Across the board I walked, bouncing slightly at the end. And then it happened.

The nightmare flashed at me as I leapt for the sky, hands reaching. I heard laughter and saw faces. I remembered to turn around in the air and I cut through the water cleanly. I was supposed to be looking for something, what, where? That feeling came over me. And then I saw him. I swam like a madman toward his small body. His cheeks were blown out and his eyes bulged open. I grabbed his hand and dragged him to the surface.

"What did I tell you?" I sputtered at Jeff the moment I had a breath of air. "If you can't swim, don't jump in."

Jeff couldn't do anything but cough and I pushed him up the ladder.

I still tasted fear at the back of my throat. It made my voice harder than I had intended. "Do you understand?"

The little fiend suddenly grinned. "Hi, Shannon. Did you see how Nicholas saved my life? Isn't he the greatest?"

I glanced up the ladder and saw her pale green eyes watching us, concerned. I decided I liked her being worried about us more than I did her dismissing me. I also realized Jeff had deliberately staged his drowning to help me. I'd have to be careful with him.

"Are you all right now?" Shannon asked.

"I'm feeling a bit woozy," I told her, holding my head. She grinned. "I meant Jeff."

"I'm okay. Only because Nicholas saved me, though."

Shannon pursed her lips. "Sure, Jeff."

"Go get my towel and wrap yourself. You're shivering," I told him. Although I hadn't planned it, that left me alone with Shannon. I wanted to say something to her. I needed to say something. Apologize, I thought, it's the only way to start over. "Listen, about yesterday. The sun must have affected my head. I acted stupid. I'm really sorry."

Her lips wouldn't commit to a frown or a smile. I wanted to kiss them.

Instead my mouth ran off. "We just moved here and I don't know anyone. Would you like to go rollerblading with me, you know, my way of making up for all the grief I caused you yesterday?"

Now she did smile. "I like rollerblading."

"You do? Good. Then you'll go?"

"What time?"

"What time, yes, that's a very good question. To be honest, I don't even know the schedule."

"How's Friday at seven? I get off at six-thirty."

"Friday would be good. I'll meet you here. Six-thirty, right?"

She grinned and nodded. For one moment, her eyes looked into mine. Then she grabbed her whistle and blew it. "Don't dive off until you know the way is clear, please," she shouted. Then she added more softly, "I've got to get back to work now."

"Sure. I understand. Friday then."

It was the same feeling I'd had when I won the high jump in a track meet the year before, when, on the last jump, I could feel the bar wobbling underneath me but in the end it held up. I'd cleared another barrier, one I'd clunked into yesterday. It was a light, high feeling, winning, getting a yes from Shannon, and it made me forget the sick fear that had clenched at my insides when I'd seen Jeff underwater.

The rest of the afternoon was carried along by that lightness. I played with Jeff and Marian — Monkey in the Middle, Shark, Tag. It wasn't like spending time with kids my own age, but it was a lot of fun. And every once in a while, I'd see Shannon watching me with a smile tugging at her lips.

When we took Jeff home, the lightness disappeared. Jeff's trusting hand in mine felt heavy. He didn't deserve to be beaten. Nobody does. I didn't feel like letting him go.

But I did. Marian and I continued past Mrs. Dobroski's house. The shrubbery looked overgrown and ragged, a storm door seemed to be off on one hinge, and paint was peeling around the wood trim. Whoever the mysterious Sasha was, the Stick Lady needed him to come and do some work.

We passed through the cemetery, carefully avoiding the large mound of earth that marked the fresh grave. I noticed Mr. McNamara shuffling back and forth from the gatehouse to a panel truck. FAIRCHILD'S TREASURES, the letters on the side read. "Does McNamara work for that antique shop near the mall?" I asked Marian.

"I think he just makes deliveries."

"Good. At least Jeff's safe . . . for now." I looked in the other direction. A bright patch of red caught my eye — near the headstone of the kid who shared my birthday, Alexander Gresko. It was a rose I discovered when I walked a little closer to it. A single red rose in a glass vase. It made me glad for him. Maybe someone was praying for his soul. Farther along, I noticed another rose in an identical vase on the grave of Mr. Dobroski. Someone liked them both. I wondered who.

"See you, Marian," I told her when we got to my section of the fence. Then I climbed over and went into the house.

A soft hum and click, click sound came from the office set up in the room next to mine. Mom at the computer. I peeked in.

"How's it going?" I asked.

Mom stared intently at the computer screen,

frowning at some figures. "If your father would only get his customers to pay in advance, we'd be fine." She looked over at me. "How was your afternoon?"

"Great. I'm going rollerblading on Friday evening."

"So Marian didn't get in the way?"

"No. She suggested it."

"That's nice." Mom's fingers rested on the keyboard and I realized she probably wanted to get back to her spreadsheet. Then another thing hit me. Accounts. Money. I didn't have any after lending mine away. Oh great, I get a date with the best-looking girl I've ever met in my life and I'm broke. I wanted to ask Mom for an advance. But her fingers were madly tap-tapping at the computer keys as she chewed her lips.

Then it came to me. There was another way, a little scary, a little dicey. But if I came out of it alive, Shannon was certainly worth it.

8

Before I left for Mrs. Dobroski's house, I looked through the junk piled in the backyard shed for some tools. I found a small green metal box Dad had bought for me back when I was around ten — my own personal toolbox. Perfect. I grabbed it and headed for the back fence. Up and over, I jumped into the graveyard and headed toward the gate.

The afternoon was ending and the summer heat had given way to a pleasant late-August warmth. In the shade of the graveyard oaks, I shivered. I stopped for a moment at the lamb tombstone, and stared at the words engraved on it.

Corey Fairchild
1985–1990

Fairchild — as in Fairchild's Treasures? I wondered. Was Corey related to the shop owner? And had he drawn the swimming pool picture I'd found in my heating vent? So what, anyway? Accidents happened. Children died whether they left a drawing in your heating vent or not.

Now I stared at the date — 1990. He'd died a while ago. Marian couldn't have known him. She said he hadn't lived in our house, which must also be true. Five year olds didn't live in group homes. But 1990, hmm, that date meant something to me — like, *in four-teen-hundred-and-ninety-two, Columbus sailed the ocean blue*, something had happened in 1990. What? What?

I continued to wrack my brain until I left the graveyard. Now I approached Mrs. Dobroski's house. The Stick Lady. I wasn't afraid, was I?

For a moment, I remembered her blade glistening in the sunlight before she stabbed at the grave. Maybe she wasn't a witch. Maybe she was a serial killer, inviting teenagers to her house to fix it up and then letting them have it.

I was approaching the flagstone walk to her house. I had to make a decision. Was she a killer or a harmless old lady who would help me pay for my date with Shannon?

Shannon. For a moment her image drifted into my mind. I saw her lips not quite formed into a smile and I wanted to kiss them. No money. I imagined her reaction

73

to that, her head tossed back and her mouth wide open with laughter. Mrs. Dobroski was a harmless old lady, I decided, and walked to the door.

The hinge caught my eye and I stopped to reach for a screwdriver. Where the hinge had come loose from the frame, the metal was rusting but I could still make the screws go back in and hold. I turned the handle of the screwdriver a few times, but before I could finish I heard a creak. The door hinge needed oiling. I looked up and saw the Stick Lady standing on the other side. I gave the screw one last turn and stood up. She opened the door.

"So good you came, Sasha." She smiled and her skin creased in a million places like worn out leather. Her eyes smiled too. It was as if little candles lit up behind them.

"Hi. I'm not Sasha."

"Ah, you don't want to be called that anymore, do you? The door looks much better, Alexander. Thank you so much."

"Alexander? Alexander," I repeated, stunned for a moment. I swallowed. "My name is Nicholas, ma'am."

"Nicholas?" The smile and all the creases stayed frozen on her face for a moment. Then they deepened. "But of course. Nicholas is a good Russian name too. Come in. Come in."

I stepped into the hallway. The walls were papered in an ornate velvet covering, the floor, hardwood like ours, was partly hidden by a cream and wine-colored carpet.

"Please, Nicholas, your shoes." She waited while I

took off my sneakers. "Step only on the red parts," she told me then as I followed her along the carpet into the kitchen.

What did that mean? I stopped and looked down.

"The white parts, you know, are difficult to clean." Mrs. Dobroski glanced back over her shoulder. I saw how she tiptoed unevenly along.

Aw, the carpet, she must have meant to step on the wine-colored parts of the pattern. I saw a flash of movement around the corner and tried to follow it with my eyes.

"Persian." Mrs. Dobroski told me as though I'd asked her a question.

Again I didn't understand what she was talking about. "The rug, ma'am?" I asked.

"The rug, yes. But also the cat. Misha, come here, you old gypsy. Come and meet Nicholas."

We stepped into the kitchen then and I saw a blue-eyed cat staring up at me from her food dish. She was pure white with long angel fur but when she opened her mouth to lick around her lips, her pointed eyeteeth gave her the look of a demon.

"A cup of decaf, Nicholas?" Mrs. Dobroski plugged in a kettle. "I have no cola, sorry."

"Decaf's fine." I looked around the small, dark kitchen and noticed a doorway lit up by a huge chandelier. "Hawh!" I gasped as something knocked against my leg with the force of a linebacker.

"Misha, stop that! You are scaring Nicholas."

Misha tiptoed away and then turned to make another run at me. Her tail flicked through the air and

I noticed the tip bent over at a strange angle. I reached down to pat her and she meowed, showing me her demon teeth again. I stroked her anyway but she slunk down in disgust each time my hand made contact with her.

"You take sugar?" Mrs. Dobroski asked me.

"No, thank you, just a lot of milk."

Mrs. Dobroski set out a couple of cups and saucers. Thin and bone-colored with large pink-red roses painted on them, they looked different from any cups or china I'd ever seen. "You want to take one? We will sit in the dining room."

I picked up a cup and saucer that looked as fragile as Mrs. Dobroski. She noticed me staring at it.

"It's Rosenthal china. Very expensive and precious to me, a wedding present from my mother."

"I can drink from a mug," I offered, suddenly feeling awkward with this tiny ornate cup in my hand.

"Nonsense. You are someone to be trusted, Nicholas. You are like Sasha. This is why I must be mixing the names." She tapped a crooked index finger at her head. "Come, come."

She led me through the doorway to the room with the chandelier. Sunlight beaming in from the window bounced off the crystal prisms, showering the tablecloth with little rainbows. We sat down around the table. "A cookie perhaps?" Mrs. Dobroski reached over to a metal tin in the center of the table and opened it. Beside the tin I noticed a vase full of red roses.

I took a wafer stick from the tin and bit into it — mocha.

"You fixed the door already."

"Actually, you could use a new door and frame, ma'am, before the winter. I just fixed it temporarily." I sounded like Dad drumming up business. How many more customers did he need so that we could afford to move away again? I sighed.

Bong, Bong, Bong, Bong, Bong! The sound startled me and I turned in the direction from where it was coming.

"You like it?" Mrs. Dobroski asked me. "It's Sophie, my grandmother clock. Another wedding present. From my mother-in-law."

"It's, it's . . ." I fumbled for the right words as I stared up and down the height of the clock. Dark cherry wood with a large brass pendulum, it had a cream-colored face with black roman numerals and brass hands.

"Ugly like my mother-in-law and noisy too! You should hear Sophie at lunch! Bong, bong, bong, bong, bong."

"Um, Mrs. Dobroski, I didn't realize it was already five. Is there something you want me to do for you?"

"Hmm, yes. Can you do the eavestrough today? I think there is a bird's nest stuck in there."

"Do you have a ladder?"

"Certainly, Sasha, I mean Nicholas. We can get it from the basement."

When I finally set the ladder up and climbed to the top, the whisk Mrs. Dobroski gave me didn't work on the wet dirt. It took me about an hour and a half to clear the eavestrough and as I circled toward the end, scooping out the muck with my bare hands, I frightened a small brown bird from its perch. It fluttered off in such a panic that it knocked into the front picture window of the house. Dazed, the bird fell to the ground and I lost track of it as something else caught my eye.

From my ladder-top view, I noticed Mr. McNamara in the graveyard giving someone a hurry up signal with his hand. And then I saw Leech lazily removing a canvas newspaper bag from his shoulder. Mr. McNamara quickly snatched the bag from him and stashed it in the gatehouse. When he came out again, he handed back an empty bag and stuffed something into Leech's hand. Money?

Leech walked away quickly, but then for some reason looked up and saw me watching him. He seemed startled but recovered quickly, smiling and waving. I turned away and nearly lost my balance. Leech meant nothing but trouble to me.

I finished the eavestrough and climbed down. Misha relaxed near the foot of the ladder, engrossed with some dark lump between her paws. "What do you have there, puss?" I asked. She was chewing now, enthusiastically. "Aw, yuck. I'm sorry I asked." She'd already eaten off the head of the little brown bird that had knocked into the window.

"Nicholas, were you calling me?" Mrs. Dobroski's head appeared at a tiny side window.

"No. I was just talking to Misha here. She's eating a bird. Is that okay?"

Mrs. Dobroski shrugged her shoulders. "There's

nothing we can do. You can't teach an old cat new tricks. Are you finished, Nicholas?"

"Yes, ma'am."

"Come inside. I will pay you."

I put the ladder in the basement and went back upstairs in time to see Mrs. Dobroski reach into a closet. Her walking stick hung there and for a second I held my breath waiting for her to snatch it up and stab me with it. When she turned to face me, smiling, I sighed.

She held a black purse in her hand. From it, she pulled out a small leather pouch with a gold clasp at the top. "Oh my," she said as she opened the pouch and peered inside. "Not enough. Come in the kitchen, Nicholas. Walk on the red spots, remember."

I tiptoed on the dark parts of the rug behind the Stick Lady.

"Reach me that soup tureen, would you?" She pointed a crooked finger to the top of the fridge. "Carefully now. Good boy."

I handed her a large bowl made of the same hand-painted china as her cups. Taking it by the long loopy handle, she removed the lid and set it on the counter. Then she grabbed something from the bowl and held it out in her fist. "Is this enough, Nicholas? You must forgive me, I don't know money."

For a moment I was nervous that she might be handing me a couple of dollars. I wouldn't have said anything. I didn't want to hit up an old lady for more money, but it wouldn't have been enough to take Shannon out.

Instead she held out a crumpled twenty dollar bill.

"Thank you, ma'am. That's plenty." I shoved the bill into my pocket.

"Would you kindly put this back?" Mrs. Dobroski handed me the tureen. I couldn't help notice the other crumpled bills at the bottom of the bowl — a couple of hundreds, some fifties and some more twenties. When she put the lid back on, I reached up and sat the tureen on top of the fridge.

"Don't forget your toolbox," Mrs. Dobroski reminded me.

"I'll come by tomorrow to oil your door, if you like," I suggested as the door creaked open to let me out. She'd given me so much money, I thought it was the least I could do.

"You're a good boy, Sa — Nicholas. See you tomorrow then."

Problem solved, money in my pocket, date with a beautiful girl — still, as I walked down the street, smelling a barbecue, ever so faintly, I felt a heaviness settle onto me. Nighttime at the Home, not something I looked forward to. As I rounded the block to head through the graveyard gates, someone stepped out in front of me.

"So you were in the Stick Lady's house," Leech sneered. "What did you see?"

"What do you mean? She's an old lady with old furniture and lots of old things lying around."

"You know what I mean. Old valuable things?"

I didn't answer quickly enough. I'm not good at lying even if it's to a jerk, and I needed time to think about what to say first.

"Ha. I'm right, aren't I? Betcha she's got silverware, and antique jewelry. Hell, she probably stuffs her mattress with money. Wait till I tell Ryan."

I thought about the soup tureen on top of the fridge and again said nothing. Maybe I should have immediately denied that Mrs. Dobroski had money or anything of value. Or told him she kept a sword in her closet, and that she would use it, given the chance. But I felt all tongue-tied and on the spot.

"I gotta get home. See ya," I finally said and left. *You hardly know her, she's not your problem*, I told myself.

The smell of barbecue became stronger and I decided this was still a good day when I saw Dad in the backyard flipping a steak.

"Just in time," he said as I climbed over the fence. "This one's for you — medium-rare. I got paid for the skylight job and thought we'd celebrate." Dad smiled. He lifted the steak onto a plate which he handed to me.

Mom sat at the picnic table with a glass of wine. "Take a potato. There's the salad," she instructed. "And by the way, Ellen Drake called." Mom paused to look me in the eye.

"What did she want?" I tried to ask lightly.

"Oh, just to say she was sorry that she missed you the other day and wanted to know whether there was any more information about the house that I needed."

"Oh."

"Nicholas."

"Yes?"

"There is no more information we need. Do you understand?"

I nodded. I understood that she couldn't know any more bad things about our house and feel happy. But I also knew that I needed to know everything, whether it made me feel happy or not.

"Nicholas, when are you going to finish unpacking your things? You're not even trying to settle in."

"It hasn't even been a week, give me a break," I argued. But she was right. I couldn't help feeling that this wasn't really home, just some rundown motel we'd check out of soon.

After supper, I headed up to my room to try. I put all my clothes away, hanging some in the closet and stacking some in my dresser drawers. That didn't make the room feel mine. Everything was too neat. I unrolled my favorite poster, a picture of a red Ferrari F-40 and held it to the wall where the white smear used to be. Nah. Over to the next wall, again no, and then the next, there just didn't seem to be a good spot in that stretch of whiteness. Finally, I just rolled the poster back up and went to bed.

Curtains or a blind would help, I thought as I stretched back and stared toward the inky blackness of my window. My mind drifted gently, pleasantly, thinking of Shannon and my afternoon at the pool. The smell of chlorine seemed part of my thoughts until it became stronger.

My heart started beating harder and faster and I felt like running. A picture of Jeff with his eyes and cheeks bulging flashed through my head. I bolted upright in bed, my stomach clenched in pain. I want, I want . . . I need — the longing, the incredible longing took possession of me. I rushed down the stairs and out the patio door, the smell of the chlorine becoming stronger and stronger.

I knew he'd be there and he was. In the center of our backyard near the pool he stood, his hands raised toward me in a pleading gesture, as though he wanted my help. But how? Why? He moved down the partly buried pool steps and then back up. I felt his helplessness and I felt something more. Sadness, overpowering sadness. It welled up behind my eyes and my throat ached. I'd never wanted to cry so badly.

I stared at the figure for a while, willing him to explain to me. I concentrated so hard my head began to throb. I could make out his eyes and his mouth now and his lips moved. "Help me," I said out loud but they were the words he had formed. He moved back into the graveyard and his shape dissolved into the night.

"I'll try," I whispered into the air.

9

Next morning, as though in a dream, I heard Mom talking to someone. Her voice drifted up from below. "Go on up. He'll be awake by now." And then I heard footsteps coming up the stairs and a knock on my door.

"Just a second, I'm not dressed yet." I threw on some cutoffs and a T-shirt and then opened the door. "Ryan?" I asked stupidly.

He stood there looking like the first day I'd met him, his eyes challenging, his mouth ready to break out into laughter. Except now his head was covered with grey stubble. He held an Expos' baseball cap in his hand and fidgeted with it as he looked around my room. "Nice, very nice. I miss our decorating job though."

"What do you mean?"

"You never saw it? Ha. Me and Leech painted the word Murderer across that wall. It was great."

"Why?"

"Something to do, you know? Art. Like Leonardo de what's-his-face. Didn't he paint a ceiling?"

"No. I meant why did you paint the word Murderer?"

"Because he was." Ryan's mouth stopped looking amused and he threw a fist into his baseball cap. "The last guy who stayed in this room, you know, Alexander Gresko."

Alexander stayed in my room, I thought. "He killed somebody?" I asked.

"Corey Fairchild. Everyone knows that."

"You knew Corey Fairchild?"

"Nah. He was in my kindergarten class but he was never allowed to play with me. Never allowed out of the yard for that matter."

"Why would Alexander kill Corey?"

"Who knows." Ryan shrugged his shoulders. "And what do you care, anyway? Listen, I didn't come here to talk about him. Here." He handed me a five dollar bill. "This is the money I owe you. I wanted to ask you to a party."

"Me?"

"Look, I know you're not exactly the kind of kid who hangs around with guys like me and Leech."

I twisted my mouth. I would've liked to disagree, but I remembered the way he swaggered around and cursed at the pool and how he yelled at Leech during the Virtual Death game. I knew he was right so I didn't answer and he continued.

"This is a kind of preppy bush party. Park supervised, you know — end of the summer, Labor Day — everyone comes. Even Shannon and her gang."

"Oh yeah?" For a moment I felt a lightness as though I was leaping into the air over the high jump. *Shannon and her gang.*

Ryan pulled out a folded piece of paper from his pocket and handed it to me. "I wrote down how to get there. It usually starts around nine o'clock and ends whenever."

I took the map from him and looked straight into his eyes. They didn't challenge anymore, they apologized.

"It's nice you take time to fool around with Jeff sometimes. Maybe you can show him . . . something different, another way . . . You know what I mean." Ryan held out his hand.

I reached out and shook it. "Thanks for the invite, Ryan. Thanks a lot."

"No problem."

I walked him to the door and watched him swagger down the driveway. Could we have been friends? He broke into houses, I reminded myself. But wouldn't I, if my father asked me to? If my father beat me? I wandered into the kitchen still mulling it all over.

"Your friend told me he was letting his hair grow back in for the winter," Mom said when I joined her for breakfast.

I made a face. I didn't want to explain that Ryan

wasn't really a friend. Instead, I concentrated on stacking pancakes on my plate.

Mom sipped her coffee. Then she changed the subject. "So, did you get all your stuff unpacked?"

"No. I put my clothes away but the walls are so . . . white, I couldn't put anything on them.

"I know what you need." Mom took a container of yogurt from the fridge and started eating from it. "New posters. My unemployment check came today." Mom smiled. "Come shopping and pick some out."

"No." I answered her through a mouthful of pancake. "I've got things to do. Tonight's my date with Shannon. Plus, I'm helping that old lady, you remember, the one I told you about the other day?"

"The one who communicates with the dead?"

"Yup. She lives across the graveyard. I promised I'd oil her door today."

"Well, I can see how that would take the whole day." Mom sighed. "So then what do you want for your window?"

"You mean like curtains?"

She nodded.

"I don't care."

She threw up her hands. "You not caring, that's the problem. This is going to be our home for a long time. We have to make it ours. Come with me!" She said it in a tone of a command.

"No!" I answered her the same way. Then I saw the look in her eyes. A flash of something, loneliness? Was she having as much trouble living in this house as I was? Had she really just wanted my company?

Too late. She left by herself and I ate the rest of my pancakes, staring out the patio window. A shadow passed near the fence and when I went to the back shed for an oil can, I half expected to see somebody.

"Marian?" I called softly. No answer. I looked toward her house and called again. Again nothing. I thought I might talk to her about my ghost and ask her about Corey.

Instead, I climbed over the fence and headed toward Mrs. Dobroski's backyard gate. Once I got to her front door, I knocked, then squeezed a few drops of oil into the hinge. "Open and close it for me, Mrs. Dobroski," I said when I saw her face in the window.

"Is that good?" she asked as she swung the door back and forth.

"Perfect," I told her.

"You want a cocoa this morning, Sasha?"

I opened my mouth to correct her and then just answered, "Yeah, cocoa would be great."

Mrs. Dobroski stared at my feet and didn't move until I removed my sneakers.

Stepping gingerly on the red pattern of the rug, I followed her into the kitchen. As I stood there waiting for her to heat up my hot chocolate, Misha swished in and out of my legs.

"How did her tail get so . . . bent?"

"Oh, it was that awful man from the cemetery. He slammed the door of his hideout on her."

"McNamara?" I asked.

"Yes. He hates animals. He told me if she kept digging up plants in the graveyard, he'd fix her." Mrs.

Dobroski's microwave beeped and she removed a cup of chocolate from it. "What could I do? Misha is a gypsy, she goes where she wants." She shrugged her shoulders and handed me the cup. "Come, we will sit." She guided me into her dining room.

"You saw him do it?" I asked as we sat down.

"Eh, mmm . . ." Mrs. Dobroski fiddled with the tablecloth now. "I heard Misha cry. She'd followed Sasha, she loved him you know. And he always walked through the cemetery, just as you do. So when she came back with her tail bleeding and bent, I knew who was responsible." Mrs. Dobroski passed me the cookie tin.

I took another mocha wafer. "But how did you know McNamara shut the door on her?"

Mrs. Dobroski seemed vague now. "She was right behind Sasha when McNamara grabbed him. Misha jumped and he kicked her. When they went into the little house, Misha screamed terribly." Mrs. Dobroski shook her head. "But nobody listens to an old woman. One who can't even remember a boy's name." She sipped at her cocoa and then put the cookie tin back near the vase of roses in the center of the table.

I fingered a rose petal that had fallen onto the tin. Blood red and velvety soft with a gentle sweet scent, the roses triggered my curiosity. "They're beautiful." I pointed at the flowers. "Are they from your garden?"

"No, I buy them sometimes for myself. A little treat. I put one on my husband's grave and one on Sasha's."

"Sasha's dead?" Had she killed another teenager?

"Never in my heart. That poor boy. You know for my husband it was his time, but not for Sasha." The corners of Mrs. Dobroski's mouth turned down sadly and her eyes glazed.

Gentle and sweet like her roses, did Mrs. Dobroski have hidden thorns? Or was she just a confused old woman? I'd seen the rose on Alexander Gresko's grave. Had she just made another mistake? "Yesterday, you called me Alexander."

"I did. I'm sorry, Nicholas. Sometimes I call Misha by my dead husband's name."

"That's all right. But you never called me that before. Who is Alexander?"

She seemed lost for a moment. "He was a good boy who lived a hard life. He never belonged in that Home, you know."

"But you said you put the rose on Sasha's grave. It was on Alexander Gresko's."

"Yes. Sasha is Alexander. A kind of short form. Like Bill for William."

"I never heard of that before."

"Every day God gives us something new to learn." Mrs. Dobroski sipped noisily at her drink.

Something landed on my lap at that moment. I felt tiny claws dig into my legs and then relax. "Meow!" Misha eyed me expectantly, showing me her demon teeth.

"Break off a piece of biscuit for her. She loves the mocha too."

Misha snapped up the last corner of mocha biscuit from my hand. When she finished eating, she nudged my hand for more. I patted her instead and she leapt to the floor again. "Is there something else you need my help with, Mrs. Dobroski?"

"So much, so much. Could you clear the yard this morning?" The candles lit up behind her eyes, the glaze disappeared.

"Sure. Do you have a wheelbarrow?"

"Everything, everything for you, Sasha. Come, we will find it together."

The rest of the morning, I raked up sticks and bits of rubbish from Mrs. Dobroski's backyard while a burial took place at the cemetery. I'd never seen anything like it before so I couldn't help watching.

A black sedan and hearse rolled up first, followed by a black van. A couple of men jumped out of the van and unloaded tons of flowers which they placed around the grave. Then a black limousine and some ordinary cars pulled up. Dressed in Sunday suits and dresses, the people from the cars gathered around the hearse and a man opened the back door. I shuddered when I saw the coffin being lifted out. Maybe after a couple of years of living here I'd get used to this kind of thing.

Six men struggled with it, shifting the weight amongst themselves until they were able to hoist it up together and follow the minister to the hole McNamara had dug yesterday. The people from the cars gathered 'round. I didn't want to seem like I was staring so I lowered my eyes but I heard the quiet, singsong voice of the minister talking too softly to make out any actual words. And then there was sobbing and I heard a kid cry, "Daddy, Daddy." I had to look up. Just in time to see a woman pick up a small boy who was kicking and screaming.

Even after a hundred years of living here, I could never get used to that, I decided. Car doors slammed and within minutes the whole thing was over. Everyone was gone, but the casket sat there alone.

Not for long. McNamara scuttled out of the gatehouse with a wheelbarrow full of sod, and a shovel. Boy, I sure wouldn't want McNamara to be the last person in the world who was around me, even if I was already dead.

He touched something which lowered the coffin. Then he lifted some turf off the large mound of dirt he'd piled up the day before, and started shoveling. I looked away and began raking again. Over and over, I heard the soft chuk sound as the shovel cut into the mound, and then the rattle of the dirt as it hit the coffin. Then there was no more rattle. I glanced over as McNamara unrolled the last sod over the grave. He scowled when he saw all the flowers but he quickly placed them on top of the sod. He scowled again when he noticed me watching him, so I turned to the twigs and paper I'd piled up and scooped them rakeful by rakeful into the wheelbarrow.

Next time I dared to look, McNamara was gone but Leech was coming up the path with his canvas bag. When he knocked on the door of the gatehouse, McNamara came out and, as before, took the bag from him, then handed him what looked like money. It was a strange way to deliver papers. I remembered Leech and Ryan's discussion Leech and Ryan about finding their own mark. What was in that bag? Whose house did they steal it from?

I wanted to pretend I hadn't seen any of it. I didn't want to get involved. What could I do about it, anyway? But how much longer could I ignore Leech's activities?

The sun hung dead overhead, cooking me. My stomach rumbled for lunch so I tapped on the back door to let Mrs. Dobroski know I was going home.

She appeared behind the window. In her hand was the duck-head walking stick. Why? I backed away quickly.

"What is it, Nicki? I was just going to go for a walk."

"Uh, um. I'm finished for today."

She pushed open the door and swung her stick around. "You've done a wonderful job. Come inside, I will pay you."

"That's okay, Mrs. Dobroski. I'll come back another day to finish. You can pay me then." Maybe the extra money would come in handy on Friday but I didn't feel like chancing it. Half of me knew she would never use the hidden sword on me, but that same half also knew there was no such thing as ghosts or dreams that left an odor on your skin.

I picked up my oil can at the front of the house and headed home. Through the graveyard I dashed and then, seeing the patch of red again, I slowed down and stopped at Alexander's grave.

Alexander Gresko
Born December 6, 1975
Died 1990
Pray for his soul

He died the same year as Corey, the kid he was supposed to have killed, that's why 1990 had twigged in my head. Was it a coincidence? And why had Alexander killed Corey? They'd been friends. At least, they swam together. *Corey and Sasha*, I remembered the childish scrawl at the bottom of the crayon drawing.

I started walking quickly again when I spotted Mrs. Dobroski following me with her walking stick. I climbed over my fence and ran into the kitchen, slamming and locking the patio door behind me. From that safe distance, I watched her.

She stopped at the fresh grave and unscrewed her stick. Then she jabbed the blade into the earth again and again until she finally seemed satisfied, cleaned the blade with her fingers and twisted it back into the wooden sheath. She nodded her head.

Maybe she thought she was killing vampires, silver blade through the heart and all that. No, that was silver bullets for werewolves and wooden stakes for vampires, I thought to myself. Well, if I could be confused, so could the Stick Lady. She had some kind of an accent, was it Transylvanian? Better vampires than teenage boys. I sighed.

Mom wasn't back yet so I thought I'd try Ellen Drake's number.

"Good afternoon, Crown Realty," a friendly voice answered.

"Hi. Could I speak to Ellen Drake, please?"

There was a strange chuckle as though the person at the other end had just heard the punch line of a joke.

"This is she." Another gurgle of laughter hit my ear. "How can I help you?"

"It's Nicholas Dilon. And I was wondering —"

She jumped in. "Oh yes. Now let me get this straight, you live in that house on Winfield?"

"That's right."

"And you stopped by for the photograph of the swimming pool while I was out."

"Yes. Do you know why it was buried?"

"Yes, I do. But your mother said she'd rather not know. Now how would that be if I told you, knowing she felt that way?"

I coiled and uncoiled the telephone wire around my finger. "Ms. Drake, there's a ghost in our backyard."

"Just a minute here. I have to tell new owners about murders and suicides in the house. Or any kind of death for that matter. But ghosts, well, people have just too much imagination, I would say."

"So he died outside."

"Who are you talking about? I said no one died inside your house. You're twisting my words here . . . Nicholas, is it?"

"Yes. Ms. Drake, my mother already told me there was an accident. It had something to do with the pool, didn't it?"

"You have to picture it. Juvenile delinquents,

diving and splashing in the water. People didn't like to see that, you know. And the Winfield Boys' Home never belonged there in the first place. Nice residential area like that. That place lowered house prices."

She wasn't denying anything. "If there's a ghost, Ms. Drake, it means someone had to have died."

Ms. Drake laughed pretty hard, too hard in fact. Then abruptly she stopped. "It's that kind of talk that keeps house prices down." Her words carried an edge to them. "Besides, who believes in ghosts? I don't, do you?"

"Yes, Ms. Drake. Since I moved to this house, I most certainly do."

10

Ms. Drake's laughter echoed in my head. She was hiding something, I felt sure. I kept seeing her standing above me in that nightmare as I pressed my face against the glass surface of the pool. An accident, maybe even a murder, a buried pool, a reappearing ghost — I only knew one person who could possibly give me some missing links.

"Marian," I called out into her backyard. When she didn't answer, I headed around the front and rang the doorbell until Dr. James opened it.

"Why, hello, Nicholas." Her eyes glittered like wet stones and she smiled a straight-arrow kind of smile. "Marian, someone here for you," she called.

Marian came down the hall. "Hi, Nicholas."

"Coming to the pool?" It was the best excuse I could think of to get her alone.

She glanced toward her mother.

"Is your room clean?" Dr. James asked.

Marian nodded.

"You brushed your teeth and washed your face?" Now she grabbed Marian's head as though her daughter was only five years old, and scrutinized her face. When she let go, Marian nodded again. "Well, you still need to comb your hair."

Marian looked at me, a wild desperate pleading in her eyes.

Geez. "It's okay. I'll wait." Marian tore away. I drum-rolled my fingers on the banister as Dr. James watched me, carving me up with her eyes as she had Marian a few moments ago.

"I'm sure you know by now that Marian is not like other girls," she began. "She's special. Do you understand?"

"Um, yes . . . no, I mean, isn't everyone special?"

"Marian is developmentally delayed." Dr. James stopped for a moment as though the weight of her words made her need a rest. *Loony neighbors* was what I'd said to Mom after meeting Marian for the first time. Now that I knew her better, those words made my skin burn.

Dr. James continued, "So I'm very protective of her and careful of the company she keeps."

I wasn't sure what she wanted from me, some promise that I would never hurt her. Instead I shrugged my shoulders and nodded.

That seemed to satisfy her and she changed the subject. "Looking forward to school, Nicholas?" she asked, the smile on her face stretching a little wider now.

"No, not really."

"Well, it will keep you busy. New school, new friends. I know Marian needs something to occupy her mind." She continued to watch me just like in the dream. I was drowning and she was smiling.

"Let's go, Nicholas," Marian said breathlessly as she bounded down the last stair.

Dr. James caught her arm then and frowned as though looking for something else to hold Marian back. "Off you go. Have fun." Dr. James turned away.

We rushed out the back door to the graveyard fence and I couldn't wait any longer. "Marian, there's a pool buried in our backyard."

"You're kidding!" Her face was easy to read. Open mouth, wide eyes, she looked genuinely surprised.

"So you really didn't know anything about it?" I asked.

"No. Why would you think that?" She climbed over and I followed.

"Because you told me about a buried treasure in our backyard, remember?" We were nearing the lamb headstone now.

"Yes, the buried treasure! Nicholas, you think that's it?" Marian spoke in the same loud, enthusiastic tone as she had in the donut shop.

I didn't want the whole world to hear, but after having watched her mother in action, I decided against shushing her. "Some treasure. It's useless now." I stopped at Corey Fairchild's grave. *Corey and Sasha.* I thought of the crayon drawing. "Our real estate agent said no one died inside our house."

Marian hurried ahead.

"Hey, what's with you? Why are you running?" I called to her.

"My mother told me not to talk about him," Marian whispered loudly.

"Please." I hesitated for a moment. "Ryan told me Alexander Gresko murdered Corey. Marian, tell me about Corey Fairchild."

"He used to live in our house before we moved in."

"Why can't you talk about that?"

Marian's voice dragged. "My mother said he was a poor boy and it was an unfortunate accident but that to gossip about it would only hurt people."

"An accident! Ellen Drake said an accident had happened at our house. C'mon, Marian, I don't want to gossip, I just have to know."

Marian shook her head and again looked back toward her house. "All right." She no longer whispered but she dropped her voice and spoke in a soft, even monotone. "My mother treated Corey in the hospital. She said they'd found him at the bottom of the pool and revived him. But it was too late. He died later on."

"That could be the accident. Was it our pool?"

Marian shook her head. "The public pool."

"If Corey didn't live or die at the Winfield Home, why would Ellen Drake keep the details of his drowning a secret?" I wondered out loud. "Unless it had something to do with Alexander killing Corey." I hesitated as we passed Mr. Dobroski's grave. "Marian, I see things at night."

She turned to face me now, her eyes even larger. "You do! Why didn't you tell me?"

I shrugged my shoulders. "Because . . . I don't know. You keep secrets too."

"Because of my mother. I didn't want to. Anyway, what do you see? The shape? Kind of lit-up looking?"

"Yes." It felt great to be able to talk to someone about it. "That's what I saw the first time. Only now I see more."

"What, what?"

"Now I can make out a face and some features. It's a boy, a ghost boy, I think."

"Do you think it's Corey?" Marian asked.

"No. He's my age. I think it's Sasha."

"Sasha?"

"Yeah. Sasha is Alexander Gresko's nickname." I walked away from Corey's grave to Alexander's headstone and paced in front of it, feeling frustrated and anxious.

"Why do you think it's Alexander?"

"Little things. Do you know, he used to sleep in my room? I found a drawing of him and Corey in the heating vent of my room."

"So they did know each other?"

"The picture was of them swimming in our backyard. Corey had done it in crayon. Look at the headstone. They died the same year."

"Why do you think Sasha comes back?"

"I don't know. He stands where the pool is buried.

Sometimes he stares at me. Other times, it seems as though he's searching for something . . . or someone. It's awful, he's so sad."

"How do you know?"

"It's as if I'm feeling whatever he is. My stomach hurts whenever he's around. I know he wants something but I can't figure out what."

"Do you smell pool when he's near?"

"Yeah, Marian. You too?"

"Uh huh. What do you think it means?" Marian sounded frightened now.

"I think he won't go away until he's satisfied. And he needs me to help him." I walked toward Alexander's headstone.

"Wait!" Marian grabbed my arm.

I jumped, expecting that she'd spotted the ghost. "What is it?"

"McNamara. He's leaving the gatehouse. I don't want to go near him."

McNamara, the bulldozer who beat up on a five year old. She didn't want to go near him. What about Jeff? I yanked my elbow away. "Fine, Marian. He's gone now. Will you come on?"

She let go of my arm and tagged along behind me. I stopped at the side of the gatehouse. "Marian, wait. Can you see over to Jeff's house? Has McNamara gone in?" I asked.

"I don't see him. Oh, wait, he's in his front yard . . . at his front door . . . now he's inside."

"Good. I'm just going to check out the gatehouse." I ran around to the door but it was barred and padlocked. I jiggled the lock just in case but it didn't budge. "Maybe I can see through the window."

Marian followed close as I walked around the back of the shed toward the only window. An insect droned around my head and I swished it away. But the drone continued, insistent, higher above me. Following the sound, I looked up and saw a grey cone shape attached to the overhang of the gatehouse.

"It's a wasps' nest," Marian whispered anxiously.

I resisted the urge to scream and tear away. Marian was afraid enough for both of us. Instead, I took her arm. "Let's get away from it, okay?"

She nodded and we moved till we were at the window. It was almost as high up as the wasps' nest. I dropped Marian's hand, stretched and stood on my toes. But it was no use. "I can't see anything."

"Here. Let me give you a leg up," Marian offered. She linked her fingers into a cradle and bent over.

I stepped on her hands and, for a moment, reached the level of the window. The inside of the gatehouse was pitch black, and the tiny window was coated with dust and cobwebs. "No use." I hopped down. "Thanks anyway," I told her. "I'll have to get a flashlight."

Marian grabbed at me. "Nicholas, don't, he'll be back, he'll catch us. I know he will. Please, Nicholas."

She was right, I wouldn't try right then. "Later then. I'm going to get Jeff, though." She looked around nervously. "You can wait here if you like, Marian."

"No. I'll come with you."

As it turned out, she was safe — McNamara's pickup was gone. Jeff answered the door with his towel in hand. "Ryan promised he'd take me swimming this afternoon, but I don't know where he went."

I took his hand and it made me feel stronger as we headed for the pool. Walking in the early afternoon sun, everything seemed brighter and sharper. Sasha might have held Corey's hand just like this once. I squeezed Jeff's gently. He could never have killed him then. Ghosts didn't exist, let alone haunt my backyard.

From a block away I picked out Shannon, sitting on the lifeguard chair, bronzed hand shading her sunglass-covered eyes. Her hair hung down her back in a thick gold braid. Bronze and gold, as Leech said, a goddess. I have a date with a goddess tonight, I told myself, trying to block thoughts of a drowning five year old from my mind.

Something buzzed near my ear and I windmilled frantically to get it away.

"Wasps don't hurt you, if you hold still," Jeff told me.

"You're right." I breathed in deeply and smiled at him. "Hey, want me to teach you how to swim, Jeff?" I asked in a forced bright voice.

"Sure!" he answered.

"All right. Just let me say hello to Shannon first."

Marian and Jeff laid out the towels and I walked over to the lifeguard chair. "Hi there. Shannon?" I had to call to get her attention.

"Oh, hi." She smiled. A row of perfect white teeth appeared. She dazzled the nightmare feeling away even though she didn't look directly at me. Dark sunglasses on, she continued to scan the pool area.

"You remember about rollerblading tonight?"

Now she slipped the sunglasses down her nose and her eyes focused on me from above them. Beautiful! "Sure, I remember. Do you mind if we grab a bite to eat first?"

"No, that'd be great." She'd handed me a different kind of problem, one that could be handled with logic. I mentally divided up my twenty-five dollars. Eight each for rollerblading, and another nine for food. I'd have to control my appetite. "Well, I'll see you at six-thirty."

"See you." Shannon leaned over to talk to another lifeguard.

Tonight I'll have her all to myself, I thought and smiled, in spite of everything else. "Come on, Jeff," I shouted to him. "Jump in."

"Oh, boy! The diving board?"

"No! Not till you learn how. I meant over here where you can stand." We both slid off the edge into the water. "Watch what I do first." I lay back in the water to show him how to float but when it was his turn, he threw himself backward against the water, his arms and legs flailing.

"Relax, hold still. Here, I'll hold you up underneath your neck. Hold his feet for a second, Marian."

She wrapped an arm around Jeff's legs to stop them from kicking.

"I get it, I get it." But Jeff's arms kept flailing around desperately.

"Not quite. Stop!" With my free hand, I gently touched his arms, quieting them. "Can you feel yourself floating?"

"Yeah. I've got it. Let me go! Let me go!"

Marian released his legs and I slipped my hand away from his body but immediately his arms and legs churned wildly at the water. As he began to sink, Jeff stood up. It was like teaching a sparkplug to swim. "You're doing great," I lied after a couple of tries, just to encourage him. "Floating's the hardest part."

"More, more," he demanded. "I want to learn now!"

"Nah, we need a rest. Look, over there's a free inner tube. Grab it. We'll play ball in the hole."

That seemed to distract him a while. His older brother never showed up. When I got fed up playing with Jeff, I told him I was going for a few dives.

"Can I dive too? You said I knew how to swim now."

I smiled at him. "No, Jeff. Stay with Marian for a while. Promise?"

He made a face but he nodded.

Each time I walked out onto the diving board, I checked for Jeff. Flailing the water around him, trying to perfect his back float, he kept his word and stayed with Marian. As I bounced, I hesitated, waiting for the terrible nightmare sensation to grip me. When it didn't, I looked to see if Shannon was watching. Not even once. Tonight, I thought, and the world felt normal, magical even, instead of on the verge of some kind of catastrophe. Up into the sky, down into the water, I shot like an arrow. I loved it.

After, when I'd joined Marian and Jeff, I noticed Shannon looking at me. When I bent down to help Jeff with the knot in the string of his bathing suit, I saw her smile. Maybe I need to take Jeff with us rollerblading, I thought. But only for a second.

It was tiring being responsible for a little wired-up kid like Jeff. He needed to be constantly moving, touching, running, finding out about things. Before closing time, I told Marian and Jeff it was time to go.

"Aw, there's fifteen more minutes left, Nicholas. Can't we stay?" Jeff begged.

Marian was already off in the women's changing room. "Give me a break, kid. I have a date tonight."

Jeff frowned.

Shannon walked over. "Bye, Jeff. See you, Nicholas."

Jeff grunted something and gave her a dirty look. I rolled my eyes, smiled and waved to her. Light and happy, I headed home with Marian and Jeff.

But as we passed near the cemetery, the magic faded. "Jeff," I asked as I saw the little stone hut, "what does your dad keep in the gatehouse? Do you know?"

"Shovels, tools and bodies," Jeff answered. His shoulders slumped as we rounded the block toward his house.

Marian gasped.

"Bodies?"

"Yeah. Dad told me never to go near the little house. But Ryan told me he saw a body in there when he was my age."

"Well, I don't think he could be right, you know. Because the bodies come in coffins in those long, black cars. Anyway, time to go, kiddo."

Now Jeff dragged his feet. "Are you coming swimming tomorrow, Nicholas?"

"Tomorrow's Saturday. I don't know, Jeff. We'll see."

"Bye," Marian called to him. She stayed at the end of the path leading to his house. I tried to look through the window to see if McNamara was around. He didn't seem to be there and his truck was still gone.

Even so, we walked back the long way. Bodies in the gatehouse, imagine. What kids will believe. *When Ryan was Jeff's age*, that's when he'd seen the body. What would that be, around five years old? If Ryan was just teasing Jeff, why would he have been so specific about his age? I couldn't figure that one out.

Instead I thought about what was in that gatehouse now. What had Leech brought McNamara in that canvas newspaper bag? I didn't feel like involving Marian so I said goodbye to her and then rummaged in our toolshed for a flashlight. At the same time, I grabbed a bucket to act as my stepladder to the window.

Back over the fence I climbed, awkwardly gripping the flashlight and pail handle. I jogged over to the hut and checked for McNamara. No sign of him, and still no pickup truck in his driveway. I felt safe stepping on top of the upside-down bucket. The beam of my flashlight lit up the thick layer of dirt coating the window but I still couldn't make out a thing. I stepped down, frustrated.

Carefully avoiding the wasps' nest, I walked around the little building to the front. There was no other way in, so I yanked at the padlock in desperation and with a soft click, it came unlocked.

I pulled open the door and looked in. There were a bunch of shovels hanging from hooks on the wall, a wheelbarrow, a stack of rolled artificial turf, a couple of pails — regular stuff for a graveyard caretaker's shed, I guess. Behind the shovels, something glinted back at my flashlight. I went over, took down the cleanest shovel and saw, on a shelf sunk into the wall, a CD player, a portable television and a computer.

"Ahem!" someone said quietly behind me.

I whirled around to see Leech dragging in a newspaper cart. Something was in the cart but it was covered by a piece of canvas.

"Saint Nick, see anything you like? Half price for you."

"Why would I want any of this junk? My father has plenty of tools at home."

"Don't make me laugh." Leech removed the canvas from his cart. A jewelry box and parts of a computer now sat in plain view. "You know what's going down here. You also know to keep your mouth shut, don't you?"

I shrugged a kind of yes.

"Sure you do. Now get outta here."

I pushed by him and grabbed my bucket on the way back to the fence. There was nothing else I could have done I told myself, glancing back. Leech was a criminal. Did I want to get myself hurt? Did I really need to get involved? Why did we have to move to this stupid neighborhood, anyway?

I slammed the patio door shut behind me.

"Nicholas? Something wrong?" Mom was holding an electric drill in her hand.

"Nah. Nothing."

"I just finished putting up your new blind. Your room looks . . . clean. Really clean," she continued brightly. "It could use a bit of you in it, but that will come, I'm sure."

"Don't count on it, Mom." I stomped up the stairs and surveyed the room. It would never, never be mine, I thought. It belonged to someone else: Alexander Gresko. What did it look like when it was his room? Did he have posters up? Or just a crayon picture that a five year old drew him? A five year old whom he later killed. I couldn't believe that. I picked up the picture from my bureau . . . Corey and Sasha. Corey and Sasha. It pounded at my head. I walked over to the window, raised the new blind and put my face to the screen. Secrets, secrets, the leaves whispered outside.

11

At six o'clock, I took a quick shower and changed into fresh jeans for my date with Shannon. I also ate a cheese sandwich and an apple so I wouldn't have to spend too much of my twenty-five dollars feeding my own face.

"Aren't you forgetting something?" Mom asked me as I headed for the door.

"What?"

"Your rollerblades." She smiled.

"Thanks," I said, feeling like a total airhead. Still there were no other thoughts pounding in my head either and that felt great . . . normal, almost. With my blades draped over my shoulder, I headed out again. I walked the long way to the swimming pool, wanting to avoid the graveyard with all its secrets for just one night.

As I strolled up to the pool gate, I saw Shannon sitting on the attendant's counter waiting for me, her long legs crossed. She wore jeans faded to the color of the sky and a torn white T-shirt. Absorbed with applying lipstick, she pursed her now strawberry red lips at a compact mirror. My heart leapt over a high jump bar.

"Hi, Shannon, ready to go?" I asked.

"Mmm. Hi, Nick." This was the first time she'd shortened my name. I decided I liked Nick when it came from her lips. Who was I kidding? I would like anything coming from her lips. "Where's your car?" She snapped her compact shut.

"I don't have one."

"Well, I meant your mom or dad's."

"Shannon, I'm not — I don't have my driver's license yet." Telling her I was too young to drive didn't seem like the most impressive opener.

"Oh." Her mouth stayed shaped around the letter. She was killing me. "I guess we can take a bus," she said as she jumped down and reached for her sports bag.

For a moment I toyed with the idea of grabbing one handle as a step toward holding hands. But, too late — she raised an eyebrow at my hesitation. We started walking toward the bus stop.

Other times when I'd seen Shannon, she'd mostly been either sitting in a lifeguard chair or I'd been in the water, so I'd never got a clear idea of her height. Now, as we walked along together, I realized she had about three inches on me. I felt relieved when the bus came right away. Now I could sit down with her and let her get to know the Nicholas that women — well, my mother and Marian, anyway — loved and adored, before my height discouraged her.

She headed for the backseat and slid over to the end. Then she stood again and hoisted the window up. I watched her upper arms tighten as she strained for a second. It wasn't like she was a bodybuilder, but I could tell she was strong and I admired that.

"That's better," she breathed when she succeeded in letting in a rush of air.

"Yeah," I answered, and then there was an embarrassing gap in our conversation. "Can we eat at Skeeters or is there some place else you had in mind?" I finally asked.

"How about Pasta, Pasta?"

"Hamburger, hamburger is fine too," I said, not understanding why she was repeating herself.

She laughed gently. "No, silly. Pasta, Pasta is a restaurant near the mall. They have an all-you-can-eat buffet. Do you like Italian?"

Do I have enough money to like Italian? I wondered. "Um, yeah, sure."

We ended up getting off the bus right at Fairchild's Treasures. I closed my eyes tightly for a moment. I won't think about Leech or Ryan, I told myself. Just for tonight. But then I couldn't help looking back at the antique bear in the window, seeing in his worn-out fur and shiny bead eyes a personality that reminded me of Jeff. And that made me think of McNamara, the graveyard and of course, our house.

"Are you always this quiet?" Shannon asked.

"Me? No. I usually shoot my mouth off." Her eyes met mine. They were such a pale green they could appear blue or grey depending on the light. "But with you," I stammered as my face grew warm, "I'm shy."

"Right," she whispered and then pushed on the door to the restaurant, holding it open for me.

"Thanks." I touched her elbow lightly.

"Smoking or non?" the waiter asked us.

"Non," Shannon answered. We followed the guy to a back booth. His knobby, hairy knees poked out of his black Bermuda shorts, and a bicycle horn hung around the collar of his red-striped shirt. He honked it twice as we sat down. "Do you want a menu or will it be the buffet this evening?"

"I'll have the buffet," Shannon answered.

I mentally multiplied the price on the sign by two and added a few dollars for pop and tip. I was about to ask for a glass of water.

"Will that be one bill or two?" Knobby Knees asked.

"Two," Shannon answered.

"Hey, I was counting on treating you," I protested. But when she shook her head, I let it go. "I'll have the buffet also," I told the waiter with relief.

Knobby Knees scribbled that down. "Go ahead and help yourself. The plates are over there," he said and disappeared.

With a sandwich and apple in me, I barely kept up to Shannon's trips to the buffet table. First plateload, I cringed when Shannon chose a non-garlic green salad with oil and vinegar dressing. Too late to dump my Caesar back. Please take the garlic bread, I thought. She picked up a couple of pumpernickel sticks instead.

"So how do you like living here?" Shannon asked during her second plate, fine thin pasta with a green herb coating.

"Here?" I repeated. I finished chewing my mouthful of tortellini but I had to swallow hard as the image of our blood-colored house came into my mind. "Fine," I lied quickly and picked up my fork again. "How do you like lifeguarding?"

"Well, it's rougher than I thought. We have to take breaks all the time to rest our eyes." A piece of angel hair hung over her lip and then disappeared into her mouth. "I'd die if anything ever happened while I was on duty."

An unfortunate accident. The words came back to me with a sudden chill. "Have you ever had a drowning at your pool?"

"Never. Not in the history of the pool."

"You're absolutely sure?"

She nodded.

Like a nail pounded over and over, the information finally hit home. If Corey hadn't drowned at the public pool, he must have died in the pool buried in our back-yard. Marian was wrong, it was the only answer. Now my spaghetti tasted flat and the lightness of the evening faded.

We ordered the Mudpie Pigout but the chocolate tasted bitter in my mouth.

"That was great," Shannon said, wiping some

chocolate sauce and the rest of her lipstick from her mouth.

"Mmmm," I answered and reached my hand across the table, reaching for lightness and normality again. I touched her hand. It felt warm and soft, and the bitter taste in my mouth melted back into chocolaty sweetness.

"It's pay day. I can get the tip." Shannon slid her hand away after a second and pulled a wallet from her sports bag.

I hesitated, stammered and fumbled with my wallet but not quickly enough. She placed a few bills in the center of the table. We paid our separate checks to Knobby Knees, I tossed back a few mints and we left.

It had been a while since I'd rollerbladed and after tying and strapping on the skates, I stumbled as a wheel caught in a wad of gum.

"Are you all right?" Shannon asked and gave me her hand to help me up.

It took me a few seconds to get my breath back but I grabbed her hand and when she smiled, I squeezed it.

"I'm fine. Perfect in fact," I told her, and from that moment on never released her hand again. We skated out into the rink.

Loud rap music pulsed from the walls, reminding me of the rock music that now played in our house of horrors. But a disco ball shattered a spotlight into a million stars that followed us as we skated and I could forget again. It made it seem as though we were rollerblading on a treadmill, suspended in a strange nighttime world of our own. That other world faded far away.

By the time the DJ put on a slow piece, my skate legs had returned and I rollerbladed backward so that I could hold both Shannon's hand and the small of her back in a kind of skate waltz. Perfect, perfect.

We rode home on the bus still holding hands.

"Do you work on Saturdays?" I asked Shannon.

"Yup. And Sundays."

"Maybe I'll come swimming tomorrow then with Jeff and Marian."

"I think it's sweet, the way Jeff looks up to you." Shannon leaned her head against my shoulder.

"He does, doesn't he?" I could feel Shannon's hair soft against my skin. I stroked it with my hand.

"And it's great that you spend time with Marian too."

"Marian's mostly okay. I can't believe she's in the same grade as I am, though."

Shannon sat up ramrod straight. "Marian's only in grade nine this year."

"Yeah," I answered cautiously. Too late, I realized what was happening.

"How old are you anyway?" Shannon asked me.

"Fifteen." I quickly added three months to my age but it didn't help.

"Ahh! I've been cradle robbing!"

"How old are you?" I asked.

"Sixteen," she snapped like a binder being shut. "You seemed so much older."

"Maybe I am. What difference does it make? Nobody has to know."

"In another week, school will start. Everyone will know."

"Nobody will care."

Shannon's arms folded across her chest and she leaned away from me. It was pretty obvious the person who mattered most cared. When she tugged on the wire to signal her stop, I stood up to go with her. I checked out the window. It was a new subdivision, fresh houses with no bad history. Like my old neighborhood. Where I'd want to live.

"Sit down." She gently touched my chest. "I'll be all right. My house is just over there." She pointed to a new, white brick, ranch-style bungalow, all brightly lit up as though on display. "You don't want to use up another token just so you can walk me that little piece."

Yes I did. I wanted to delay the bad dreams for a while longer but she didn't want my company. It was clear. So instead I reached over to kiss her. She didn't pull away but it was a dry, short, unfeeling peck. "Goodbye," I told her because that's what it was.

I stepped off alone at my bus stop. The moon was a huge silver ball and the sky was pure black, speckled with a million stars, reminding me of the better part of the evening when I'd been rollerblading at Skeeters, Shannon's hand in mine. Now that I had to walk the last couple of blocks home on my own, I could feel a heaviness settle over me.

Crickets, millions of them, chirped shrill from the lawns around me. A man with a huge panting dog jogged toward me. Both he and the dog had shaggy grey hair that spilled over their eyes. Owner/dog look-alikes. The dog's legs stretched long as he ran, the man's bent like pistons at work. The dog's ragged row of white teeth opened in a grin at me.

I moved to the inner edge of the sidewalk but still felt the animal's hot breath against my leg as it jostled past.

"Nice night." The man grinned at me too, looking even more like his hound from hell.

The *neighborhood* from hell, I thought as I turned into my driveway. My stomach began to ache — too much to eat, hard disappointment or simple dread. Then the ache increased. Was I getting an ulcer? I inhaled deeply through my nostrils. No, it wasn't an ulcer, I realized. My nose hair sizzled together as my eyes began to water. Chlorine. I glanced back, but the hound and his master jogged with their same rhythm. They'd noticed nothing. It was only me and my house of horror.

I headed for the back, realizing by now I was being summoned.

12

From somewhere I heard a dog bark, sharp and warning, then a yelp and then a door slamming. Step by step, I continued forward, through the back gate onto the patio. The chlorine smell, heavy and hot, sucked the breath from my lungs. My chest pounded, my eyes flamed. I grasped my throat and stopped. I couldn't move any closer.

Every blade of grass stood straight and frozen white in the moonlight. The crickets fell silent.

He stood at the pool steps, waiting patiently, his shadow long across the whiteness. His features were blurred and his body, if you could call it that, ended just where his feet should have been.

"Sasha?" I whispered softly.

No answer. Tears blurred my vision and over-whelming sadness, deep, black regret — wave after wave of his emotions — swept over me. The ghost turned and stepped down into the pool.

"Corey?" he called but the words came from *my* lips. I whispered the name, as though the chlorine had sucked my voice away. My heart stopped and images from all my nightmares whirled through my head.

High up and far away on a diving board, I was look-ing down, dizzy and sick. Then a jolt of energy buzzed inside me and the sound of water rushed past my ears as I dove. Bubbles burst all around me. Desperate flail-ing. Where was he? Where was he? I flailed one way and then the other. Nowhere, nowhere. I needed air. I wanted to throw up, my stomach hurt so much now. Up, up, to the surface. I clutched at my throat. Jeff's face, with bulging cheeks and eyes, appeared before me.

But I was howling with Sasha's voice, "Cor-eeeey!" Sasha floated up the stairs, over to the hole in the fence, back to the pool steps again, down and then up. Anxious pacing. "Let me go, let me go. I have to help him. I have to." I sobbed out his words.

My nightmare came back to me. The glass wall. I couldn't breathe and I couldn't move.

His nightmare. *Life and death. I can save him, but only if he lets me go.* "Let me go," I screamed with his words. "He'll drown if you don't."

"Oh, no. No, no, no!" His sobbing from my lips. A flash of an image. A grey stone wall. Impact. Warm blood trickling from my mouth and ears and more deep, black regret. "If only," I whimpered.

Sasha turned toward the graveyard, freeing me to speak on my own again. "If only what? Tell me," I begged. "Tell me! Who drowned? It was Corey, wasn't it?" My heart felt heavy, like an anchor. "Don't go! Please, I don't know how to help yet."

Sasha turned one last moment to face me.

"Stop him." Once my lips had formed those words, his words, my body became free to move.

Stop him. Those words rolled endlessly over in my head. I wanted to shut them out as I wanted to shut out their message. But I couldn't. Who did Sasha want me to stop? Who could I stop? My eyes rested on the grey stone gatehouse. McNamara? He beat Jeff and he stored and sold stolen goods. Somewhere inside, I'd known I needed to stop him the moment I'd heard Jeff screaming. But how did McNamara connect with Sasha?

I'll find out, somehow I'll find out, I promised myself and returned to the house and got into bed.

Too soon it seemed, I heard Mom's voice calling me. "Breakfast, Nicholas. I made your favorite. Hurry up!"

Saturday bacon and eggs, I could smell it. I could also hear rock music coming from the radio. I'd never realized before how much I'd come to expect classical music in the morning. The music and nightmare memories rattled me as I threw on some clothes, brushed my teeth and headed for the kitchen.

"Here you go!" Mom set my eggs in front of me.

"Dad gone already?" I asked as I sat down and grabbed some toast from the plate in the center of the table. I thought that maybe I could have discussed McNamara's storehouse of stolen goods with him.

"Yes. Another job, thank goodness." Mom sat down and nibbled at a slice of toast.

I watched her, wondering if I could talk about my ghost with Mom.

"You don't like classical music anymore?" I decided to ask the safest question first.

"Yes, but it doesn't feel right to play it here." Mom looked around uncomfortably, almost wincing. "I like loud, hard music in this house, you know?"

"Yup," I answered, noting the purple circles under her eyes. Knowing made it worse for her and I couldn't make her more unhappy with our home. It wasn't fair. So I didn't say anything else.

"How did the date go?"

"Great, until she realized I was fourteen."

Mom smiled. "Ah, the older woman, like father like son. Did you tell her I was three years older than your father?"

I shook my head. "You're not exactly Romeo and Juliet anyway," I said after I swallowed some orange juice.

Mom laughed. Compared to Ellen Drake's laughter in my nightmares, it was like the sound of soft sleigh bells. Bells I hadn't heard for a while and missed. "Sure we are. Maybe not to you," she said. "Are you going to the pool today?"

"Not today. Maybe not ever. I'm waiting till I recover my pride."

"Well then," Mom started excitedly, "school starts Tuesday. Let's get some clothes for you." She fingered the keyhole in the cutlery drawer and shook her head.

"Then you can help me pick out some wallpaper to brighten this kitchen."

It's impossible, I thought to myself as I stared up at another set of whitewashed walls and shrugged. "You're the decorating expert."

"But if you have input, maybe the house will appeal to you more. And you need school clothes."

"Maybe Friday. I still have some work at Mrs. Dobroski's. She owes me money too."

So Mom took off for the mall again alone. It wasn't like her to shop so much. Could she not face staying at the house by herself?

I felt bad for her but if I could help Sasha find peace, it would help us all.

Staring out the patio window into the graveyard, I saw McNamara setting up a sprinkler near the fresh grave.

Stop him. Stop him from what? Fencing stolen goods? But how? Should I call the police when McNamara received another "paper delivery" from Leech? Would they believe me? Would they need proof?

First things first. Dobroski's house, I told myself, rinsing off my breakfast dishes.

On my way through the cemetery shortcut, I spotted Mrs. Dobroski at her husband's grave. Not wanting to disturb her, I stood on the path nearby, waiting for her to look my way.

"Hawh! Oh, Nicholas, you gave me a fright. You did so look like Sasha in the light." She raised a hand to shield her eyes.

I couldn't help staring at her cane. "Mrs. Dobroski, I thought I would clean up your front yard today."

"It is good, very good. I worried you would never come back."

I wondered about that for a moment. Had she thought something would happen to me? Nah, I shook that thought away. Maybe she realized how afraid I'd been of her the last time I'd seen her.

She didn't seem at all frightening now as she leaned heavily on her cane, walking beside me.

We were nearing Alexander's tombstone. "Why do you stab the graves?" I finally blurted out and waited for her reaction.

"Me?" Her hand shook as she raised her cane, looking thoughtful. She unscrewed the cane and pulled out the sword. Sunlight flashed off the blade.

I gasped and stepped back. The fear returned immediately.

"What is the matter with you, Nicki? You are nervous? I don't stab the graves. I am checking."

"Ma'am?"

"See here. This is the mark for three feet." Without warning, she jabbed her sword into Alexander's plot. It sunk past her mark. "This one he did properly, you see. If I hit the coffin before the mark, I know the hole has not been dug properly."

"You're measuring the depth of the grave, Mrs. Dobroski? But why?"

"Because that miserable man — he's so lazy." She pulled the sword out of the ground, and shook it at the gatehouse. "I watched him dig my Albert's grave. He did it with so little care." Mrs. Dobroski's eyes filled with tears.

"So you checked with your cane?" I couldn't believe this, she was so bizarre.

"Yes. The grave is supposed to be six feet deep. Three for the coffin and three for the earth on top."

"Did you catch him?"

"Not only once! The church told me for two graves they will send the health inspector and my Albert will be buried properly. But the next time I caught him, they told me the rule has changed. Only two feet of earth on top of the coffin." Mrs. Dobroski shook her head and as she did, a tear flung onto Alexander's grave.

We both stared quietly at the tombstone. *Pray for his soul.*

I waited for Mrs. Dobroski to compose herself and then I couldn't wait any longer. "Ma'am, do you think Alexander killed Corey?"

"My Sasha? Never." Mrs. Dobroski's whole body shook. Her lips moved as though she were going to say something but she didn't. More tears fell. "Come home with me, Sasha," she said after a moment.

I didn't bother correcting her. I just nodded and followed her out of the graveyard.

"You'll have a decaf or a hot cocoa?" she asked when we entered her bungalow.

"Just a glass of milk, please. It's kind of hot for coffee."

"I am suddenly feeling very cold." She hung up her walking stick on the hook inside the closet door and then removed a shawl from the top shelf. She shook as she drew it around her shoulders. Her breathing became loud and raspy.

"Are you all right?" I asked her.

She acted as though she hadn't heard me. "A milk, you said?" She seemed far away as she poured me a glass. She fixed herself an instant coffee and we sat down in the dining room.

I noticed the roses in the center of the table had purpled and lost most of their petals. They lay dried out and scattered around the vase. Most people would have thrown them away. Why hadn't Mrs. Dobroski? Too tired to bother, too forgetful? She seemed so vacant sometimes, could I take anything she said at face value?

"Please." Mrs. Dobroski pushed the tin of biscuits toward me. It was close to the vase and maybe she'd noticed me staring in that direction.

I took out a wafer and immediately broke off a piece for Misha, leaving it on my lap. "You said Sasha would never have hurt Corey," I started gently.

"Corey?" she repeated tonelessly.

"Yes, the little boy who lived next door to the Home." I felt Misha's sudden weight on my lap then and waited as she scarfed the piece of wafer. She allowed me to pat her for the first time. "Sasha knew Corey, didn't he?"

"Oh, yes." Mrs Dobroski sipped at her coffee and stared blankly ahead. When I had almost given up on her, she finally spoke. "Sasha loved swimming, you know. And one day when he was in the pool, he heard a voice calling him." She stopped talking for a moment as if to concentrate on her breathing. "It was the little boy."

"Corey?"

"Corey, that is correct. But he was not calling Sasha, he was speaking to his imaginary friend." Mrs. Dobroski sipped at her coffee again and I waited patiently for her to continue. "Poor little boy. Can you imagine anyone being that lonely?"

I smiled. "Actually, I had an imaginary friend too, when I was little."

"So you understand. Sasha did too. You are both very much alike." She took a few deep breaths. "Sasha was friendly with this child. In fact, the last time I saw Sasha he was going to see him. He could never kill this Corey."

"When was that Mrs. Dobroski?"

"I don't remember, exactly. We heard a crash. Somebody had broken the back window. Sasha ran outside to check."

"And?"

"And that was the last time I saw him."

"You didn't go outside to see what happened?"

"I'm an old lady. What could I do? They were big boys and he chased them. Misha was just a kitten but she ran after."

"Mrs. Dobroski, if you saw him chasing these big boys, you must have gone outside and seen Sasha again."

Mrs. Dobroski didn't seem to hear me. "It was terrible you know, the crash, the glass everywhere. Sasha running, running. After those boys." She gasped for air now. "And then I heard yelling and a terrible cry." Shaking her head, Mrs. Dobroski spoke softly as if to her hands instead of me. "And when Misha returned her tail was broken." She pulled out a white handkerchief and blew into it. "Don't be angry with me, Sasha, please. I'm just an old woman."

"Don't worry," I said gently. "I'm not angry with you."

Mrs. Dobroski got up slowly. "Come and get the soup tureen, Nicholas, I will pay you for the yard now."

I walked back into the kitchen and reached on top of the fridge for the big ornate bowl. "Here."

She took off the lid and pulled out a fifty dollar bill.

"That's too much, Mrs. Dobroski. Even for both the front and backyards. Ten dollars would be fine."

"Listen to me, Nicholas. I need to go to the hospital for a few days. I want you to look after Misha and the house for me. Could you do that?"

"Um, uh, when?"

"Monday I go in. Friday I will be home."

I looked at the bill in my hand, wanting to return it to her and say no.

"Please. I have no one else for Misha and she likes you."

"Sure," I finally answered.

"Good. Thank you so much. Here is the key."

She handed it to me and I pocketed it along with the fifty dollars. "I guess I'll get started on the yard then."

Misha followed me outside. She attacked my hands as I pulled weeds from the flagstone. I dangled a dandelion in front of her face and she batted at it with her paws. When she leapt on my arm with her claws extended, I called it quits. "Look, I'm bleeding, puss. Go 'way. I need to work."

After a couple of hours, the yard was cleared and I knocked on the door just to let Mrs. Dobroski know. No answer. I waited for a bit and then turned the doorknob. The door opened. I should tell her to keep her doors locked, I thought. I tiptoed through the house on the red parts of the carpet and found her asleep on her bed, her mouth partly open and a rattling snore coming from her lips. Backing out of her room, I continued out of the house, locking the door behind me.

"What were you doing in the old bat's house?"

I turned around to face Leech who was standing on the porch. "I'm helping her . . . look after things."

"Sure, sure. You're real good friends. The crazy old witch and Saint Nicholas. Maybe we can work together too."

"Not in this lifetime, Leech."

"Oh no?" He shoved me hard, pushing me to the ground. "You sure about that?"

Ignoring him, I slowly picked myself up and wiped off some pebbles stuck into my elbows where I'd landed. "I'm absolutely positive," I said quietly and then just walked away.

13

Still rubbing at my elbows which were grey and sore, I walked home the long way. A block ahead of me, I spotted a tall, slim figure. She turned around and waved.

"Hi, Nicholas. You going swimming this afternoon?"

"No, Marian, I'm not."

She waited till I caught up and moved to one side of the sidewalk, giving me room next to her. "What's wrong?"

"Nothing you can help me with." I dropped my hands away from my elbows as I strolled alongside of her.

"That's probably true." Marian smiled sadly, then

jumped up suddenly, ripping a leaf off a tree. I thought I saw her face crumple for a moment as she skipped ahead.

Had I hurt her feelings? That would probably make one million and one times now. Only, since my date with Shannon, I knew what it felt like. I ran a couple of steps to catch up. "Look, Marian. It's about Leech and, well . . . Ryan, too."

"They're in trouble?"

"They are trouble. They break into houses. And you know how I wanted to look in the hut? That's where they store the stuff. McNamara buys it from them and takes it to Fairchild."

Marian stopped and tossed the leaf to one side. "Corey Fairchild's dad? The man who sold us our house owned an antique shop."

"It must be him then." That made me hesitate for a moment while the information sank in. "Anyway, so now Leech is pressuring me to help him break into Mrs. Dobroski's home."

"Nicholas!" Marian's eyes grew to moon size.

"Don't worry. I don't rob people's houses, Marian. Besides, Mrs. Dobroski trusts me. She even gave me the key to look after her place while she goes into the hospital."

"You talk to the Stick Lady!" Marian hung back, even more shocked.

"Yes. I cleaned her gutters and her yard."

Marian still stood frozen.

"Okay, so she's a weird old lady. She isn't dangerous or anything and I like her."

Now I was ahead of Marian and she strode quickly to catch up. "Maybe you should tell your mom about Leech and Ryan," she suggested.

"I don't know. I just want to ignore them, I don't want to snitch."

"But then you'll be helping them."

I frowned. "But I'll stay in one piece," I said, touching my elbow for a second. "You know how I said I feel the ghost's feelings? It's more than that. He speaks to me, through me, actually. Last night he told me to 'Stop him.'"

"Who does he mean?" Marian asked.

"Who knows?" I shook my head and kicked a rock on the sidewalk so hard my foot hurt. "Maybe it's Leech. Sasha was friends with Mrs. Dobroski. Maybe he wants me to prevent them from robbing her. And there's another thing."

"What?" Marian asked.

"Corey must have drowned in our backyard."

"But my mother told me . . ."

"She lied. Shannon says there's never been a drowning at the public pool." I paused for a moment. "You know how Ryan says Sasha killed Corey?"

"Yes, but Corey died at the hospital. My mother said his brain didn't have enough oxygen."

"Well, I can't believe it either. Not the way Mrs. Dobroski talks about him. Not the way he stands at the edge of the pool at night and cries." When I caught up to the rock I'd kicked, I picked it up and threw it hard against a stop sign. It dented the S. "This is driving me crazy. I need to find out more, Marian, only how?"

"Why don't we go to the library?" We were almost at Marian's house now.

"Yeah, sure, we'll look under G for Gresko in the encyclopedia."

"No, silly." Marian smiled. "Last year I had to do a project on the history of an important building in our town and the librarian helped me find a story about the grand opening of our mall. It was on microfilm. They keep all the newspapers on microfilm."

I stopped walking and turned to look at her. I had to shake myself; this was Marian talking. "I could look at newspapers around the time Corey died."

Marian nodded and grinned her gap-toothed smile.

"You're a genius, Marian!"

Her face flushed. "We have to take the bus, it's in the mall."

"Okay. Let me grab something to eat and we'll go."

"Sure." She waved as I dashed away.

Mom was studying wallpaper samples when I came in, wincing with the effort, her fingers drumming to the beat of the loud music blaring from the radio.

"Anything to eat around here?" I asked as she held one sample up, frowning.

"Pizza Pops in the freezer. Hmm. Do you think this one is too dark?" It was a sombre blue, almost black, with tiny pinpricks of white circling pink dots. The pink dots were actually roses.

"It's perfect," I said. Perfect for a funeral parlor or a home for young offenders.

"Make me a couple of pizzas too." Mom held up

another sample. This one was white with large friendly blue and red flowers. Up against our wall the flowers seemed to be mocking — big blue and red mouths that laughed at us.

I tossed four Pops on a plate and stuck them in the microwave. My elbows stung and I wiped sweat from my forehead. "Mom, I'm going to grab a shower. Can you watch these?"

She nodded absently and I took off. The cool water felt good on my elbows and forearms, but the dirt wouldn't wash away. I kept rubbing till I realized the grey was a bruise forming. *Leech, that stupid jerk.*

The shower didn't cool me down for long. The moment I stepped out of the stall, the heat pressed against me, making me feel woozy. When I returned to the kitchen for my Pizza Pops, Marian and Mom were sitting together, eating them. The smell of the sauce usually made my mouth water but today it made my stomach flip-flop.

"Hi." Marian smiled brightly.

"Hi." Her face blurred in front of my eyes for a moment.

"Don't worry. There's more in the microwave." Mom tilted her head and raised an eyebrow. "Marian says you're going to the library to look up newspaper articles."

"That's right." I frowned at her, trying to discourage the fifth degree. The microwave beeped and I removed my lunch.

"So, Mom," I said, purposely changing the subject, "did you ask Marian which wallpaper she likes?"

"Good idea! Marian, what do you think?" Mom stood up, holding her two samples against the wall.

I picked at my pizza, the heat having pretty much taken my appetite away.

Marian agonized over the wallpaper. "They're both pretty." She hesitated, her mouth hanging open.

I wiped my mouth and chucked most of my lunch into the garbage. "Let's go," I told her, trying to save her the tough decision.

"I like the white paper with the big flowers. I think," she quickly added. Then she shrugged her shoulders and left with me.

The fumes from the bus and the lurching stops made me feel sick. The windows around us were all stuck so there wasn't any air. At the library, the air conditioning didn't seem to be working either. It seemed even hotter and stuffier than on the bus.

A thin woman with spiky black hair and oversized red glasses looked up from the reference desk. "Hello, Marian. How can I help you?"

"Ms. Williams, can we see *The Journal* for the entire year of 1990?" Marian looked at me.

I thought for a moment. "Maybe just the summer. When do people usually open their pools?"

"How about I give you June through to Labor Day?" The librarian adjusted her glasses. "Go sit down. I'll bring them to you."

Marian flicked the light switch on the microfilm

projector. Then she placed the first reel Ms. Williams brought us on the spool, threading the film over to the other spool.

At first, Marian moved the film slowly. Even so, the print swam as I tried to follow it. My stomach churned.

"You can skip the Lifestyles section," I said, shutting my eyes for a moment. "They wouldn't put a drowning in there."

She pressed a button and the film whirred by. I shook myself and trained my eyes back on the screen. Reel one, reel two, reel three. "Do you think we missed it?" Marian asked as we tried the fourth reel.

"Geez, I hope not." I swallowed hard to keep my Pizza Pop from backing up into my throat.

"Hold on. What's that?"

Marian rolled back the film inch by inch until it came to the headline I'd spotted.

TRAGIC DROWNING

Five-year-old Corey Fairchild died late last night after an earlier poolside resuscitation at the Group Home for Juveniles on Winfield Drive. It appears the boy crept through a hole in the fence between his yard and that of the neighboring Home's. Eric Fallows, Winfield Home supervisor, administered C.P.R. and was able to get the youngster breathing again. Corey never regained consciousness, however.

Ellen Drake, local real estate agent and victim of the fifth break-in since the opening of the Home, recently circulated a petition to close the Winfield Home down. "What will it take?" she demanded when asked for a comment. "We've had robberies. Now a drowning. When will it end?"

The words blurred in front of me. It was all too much. I couldn't breathe, the sweat glued my T-shirt to my skin. Hot, I was so unbearably hot. Break-ins, break-ins, the words tumbled around in my head and I thought about, Leech and Ryan. "The hole in our fence — who made it?" I wondered out loud. I put a quarter in the slot and pressed Print. Marian caught the copy as it came out of the machine.

"Maybe there's something on Sasha's death. Do you want to keep scrolling?" I asked Marian.

She nodded. I tried to focus. More print swam by and the screen began to swirl in front of my eyes. "I can't anymore," I finally told Marian.

She shrugged her shoulders and looked up at the librarian who bustled over. "Problems with the machine?" she asked.

"Not exactly."

"What do you have there?" Ms. Williams asked and Marian trustingly handed over the article. Ms. Williams frowned and shook her head as she read. "Corey Fairchild, that was such a shame. You know he used to come in for story hour. But he caught a bad cold and his mother wouldn't bring him anymore." Ms. Williams shrugged. "And then he drowned. No one could believe it. She was so protective of him." She handed the article back to Marian. "So what is it you're having problems with?"

"We can't find anything on Alexander Gresko's death. Do you know anything about it?"

"What is this all about? Are you having problems with the ghost?"

"You know about him?"

"I've never seen him, but people have told me." Ms. William's forehead creased for a moment. "Comes out of the graveyard at night and just drifts near the Winfield Home. Alexander Gresko, that who you figure he is?"

We nodded.

"He was the runaway, wasn't he? I think they found his body around Christmas." She stood up. "I guess you want the December reel."

"Yes, please, Ms. Williams," Marian answered. She took over now.

More whirling print and my head spun along with the words until Marian found the small article noting his death.

BODY OF RUNAWAY FOUND

A body discovered on the outskirts of town yesterday by a man walking his dog has been identified as Alexander Gresko, fourteen-year-old former inmate of Winfield Home who disappeared Labor Day. First reports indicate death occurred as a result of skull fracture. Dental records were needed to confirm identity because of advanced decomposition and because no next of kin were available.

An investigation is underway and an autopsy has yet

to be conducted to determine exact cause and time of death.

Charged with being an accessory to burglary in 1987, Gresko had been in Winfield since the beginning of the summer. His mother and stepfather live in Germany and could not be reached for comment.

An accessory to burglary, what did that mean exactly? While Marian made a copy of this article, I searched through a huge dictionary open on a podium nearby. Skimming through the definitions, I found the one I wanted. Accessory in law. I read it out loud. "'A person who helps an offender against the law, without actually taking part in the commission of the offence.'" My stomach cramped. If I ignored what Leech and Ryan were doing, would I be helping them like Marian said? Would that make me just like Sasha? An accessory to a crime?

"Is there something about the investigation?" I asked her.

She scrolled further through. "I can't find anything. Do you want to look, Nicholas?"

"It's making me sick. I can't anymore," I told her, gripping the podium to steady myself.

Marian looked over to Ms. Williams' desk. "Do you want me to ask . . .?"

I nodded.

Marian walked over to her desk, the squeal of her sneaker soles echoing loudly. I followed more slowly, weaving between tables and chairs.

"Ms. Williams," Marian began and the librarian

looked up from a book she had been writing in. "We were wondering about the investigation into Alexander Gresko's death but we can't find it in the paper."

"Maybe there wasn't a story about it. Why don't you call the owner of the home? Mr. Hendricks. He still practices law here."

"Would he tell us, do you think?" Marian asked.

"I don't see why not. It would be a matter of public record. The phone books are right over there." Ms. Williams pointed.

Marian rushed over to the shelf and lifted down the right volume. "There are five Hendricks in here," she told me when I caught up to her in the phone book corner.

"Let me see. It's the one in bold — Hendricks, Thomas. Barr. The barr. means lawyer, I think. Could you take the number down, Marian?"

She scribbled it on a slip of paper. "There's a pay phone at the door. But, Nicholas, you have to phone."

I wanted to lie down and stop my stomach from rolling but I nodded. My last quarter went into the slot and I pressed in the number.

"You have reached the office of Thomas Hendricks, attorney at law," a toneless voice announced. "Unfortunately, we are closed right now but would be pleased to address your concerns between the hours of nine to five, Monday through Fridays. Thank you. You may leave a message at the tone."

I hung up the receiver. "We'll have to wait till Monday, I guess. Listen, I'm coming down with something, Marian. Okay if we just go straight home?"

"Sure, Nicholas."

We caught the bus and rode silently, the movement rocking me. My legs and arms grew heavy, my eyes wanted to close. A sense of urgency startled me awake at our stop.

"You fell asleep. Are you okay?" Marian asked.

"I don't know. I feel like there's something important I have to do."

"Uh huh. I'll walk you home." She took my arm and I felt grateful. "Hope you feel better soon," she told me when we reached my door.

"Thanks," I answered weakly. As I walked into the house, the smell of cooked broccoli and roasting pork made me gag. Stompin' Tom Connors wailed loudly from the radio, something about blue eyes stealing his heart. I knew how he felt. Still, my eardrums throbbed. I needed to lie down badly. As I headed past the kitchen, I noticed the cupboards were now gaping open. It jolted me for a moment. "Mom?" I called.

Dad walked into the room then, whistling along to the wailing. He held a screwdriver in his hand with which he proceeded to remove another cupboard door.

"Did you know about Dad's surprise?" Mom called from behind me in a pleased voice. "No more keyholes, won't that be great?"

"Great." Looking at the black holes where the cutlery drawers used to be, I wasn't sure.

"Supper's almost ready," Mom added.

"None for me. I've got some kind of bug." I went directly upstairs and fell into bed. The room spun

142

around with my stomach but, thankfully, I dozed off.

Then suddenly, a familiar sense of urgency jolted through me and I was running through a dream haze of greyness.

My feet pounded along a path through the graveyard; I felt and heard them thud against the hard ground. There was a louder drumming vibrating through me, and a rhythmic soft *hawh, hawh* — my own heartbeat and breathing, I realized. *Faster, faster, I have to get there, I have to get there.* The headstones became a blur on either side of me. My heart drummed harder and my breathing became noisier. *Stop him, stop him!* Who? Who? Some instinct told me that when I reached the end, I would know.

14

A gentle knocking woke me the next day. I sat up slowly, every joint complaining. My stomach felt caved in and sore, and the desperation and frustration of my nightmare made my head ache. Wiped out, I felt irritated with the world.

The door to my bedroom cracked open slightly and Mom peeked in. "Nicholas, are you all right?" she asked.

I breathed in and out heavily a couple of times. "I've been better." The words were hoarse and raspy.

"Well, I don't know if you're up to it, but I brought you some toast and tea."

"Thanks, I'll try."

She placed the tray in my lap and sat down on the edge of my bed, waiting expectantly.

I sipped at the tea. After a couple of swallows, I tested my voice again. "Is Dad around? I need to talk to him."

"He should be in a little later. He's quoting a job this morning. Somebody wants a new roof."

"Dad's never done a roof before, has he?"

"No, but he has a friend he's going to call to help him. With the age of the houses in this neighborhood, he figures he'll never be out of work if he takes on roofing."

"How much more work does he want? He's already gone every day of the week." Stupid dreams, stupid house, stupid contracting business — I hated all of it.

Mom put her hand on my forehead and frowned. "He wants to put something away in the bank in case . . ." She hesitated, her mouth twisting around as though she was strangling off the end of her sentence. She shifted her gaze away from my eyes.

"In case what?"

"Oh, I don't know, Nicholas. In case things don't work out."

There was only one "thing" as far as I was concerned. The house, the Amityville Horror. I nibbled at the dry toast, angry with her. Why didn't she just spit it out? She hated this place as much as I did.

"Nicholas," Mom started again. "I was doing the laundry and found this in your pocket." She held out the crumpled fifty dollar bill Mrs. Dobroski had given me.

"Thanks," I said taking it from her.

She watched me for some other reaction. "What you wanted to talk to Dad about, does it have something to do with that money?"

"No," I answered sharply. Mom and I had always been straight with each other but because she'd been holding back on me lately, I didn't want to share every moment of my life with her either.

"Okay," she answered softly, making me feel bad.

"I got the money from Mrs. Dobroski. I told you I was working for her."

"What did you do for her? Run drugs?"

"No!" Again I answered too sharply. Too late. I realized she hadn't meant a thing by it. I took a deep breath. "Mrs. Dobroski's going into the hospital tomorrow and I'm supposed to feed her cat and look after her place while she's there."

"Well, that's a good way to make money for your back-to-school clothes. Friday, we're going shopping."

"Great," I snapped and drank the rest of my tea noisily.

Mom took away the tray as she stood. "If you're up to it later, come downstairs, I'll make you something more substantial."

"Sure," I told her and then slunk back under the covers.

I slept on and off most of the day. Something about sleeping in broad daylight helped to chase away the nightmares. When I heard Dad's voice later, I made myself go downstairs.

The cupboards still lay open and exposed, the drawer slots black ugly cavities gaping above them. Dad stood at the stove stirring something that smelled good.

"Gee, Dad. How long are we going to have to look

at this?" I gestured at the cupboards. It wasn't what I'd meant to say at all, but I couldn't help myself.

"The doors and drawer faces haven't come in yet. I just finished the first part of the job to save time. Another couple of weeks, I expect."

I shook my head and blew out some air in disgust. "Where's Mom?"

"Out to get some ginger ale. She thought you might need some for your flu."

"Dad, can we talk?"

He grimaced. "What, more complaints?"

"No, not exactly."

"All right," he said, pulling out a chair for himself. I sat down opposite him. "Shoot."

"I know some kids who are breaking into houses."

"You're not involved, are you?"

"No!" I answered. By the speed of his question, I figured Mom must have discussed her fifty dollar worry with him.

"Good!"

"Yeah, but, Dad, doesn't knowing about it involve me somehow?"

"True enough." His mouth twisted around for a bit. He scratched the back of his head. "I guess the most important thing is to stop them."

Stop them. His words made me think of Sasha at the edge of the pool.

"But how, Dad?"

"Have you tried to talk them out of it?"

I rubbed my bruised elbows. "Sort of. That is to say, I really don't have that much influence on them."

"Well, then it seems to me you have to go to the police." Dad sighed. "The thing is, sometimes kids brag about something that they don't really do. So you want to approach the police with hard facts. Which house did they break into? When? Are they maybe wearing something they took from a house? Do you know anything like that?"

I shook my head.

"Is it possible you'll find out anything like that? I mean, without getting yourself hurt?"

"I don't know. I can try."

"I'll go with you to the police right now if you like. They may suspect these kids or even have a file on them already, but they need proof to arrest them." He paused and looked at me for a moment. "What'll it be, Nicholas?"

"Let's wait."

"Your decision. But if you change your mind, let me know. And Nicholas, you know your mother is always there for you if you need her too. Right?"

I shrugged my shoulders and then nodded.

"Now I'm supposed to make you chicken noodle soup."

My head still hurt, but the rest of my body felt a bit better and I managed to eat a few helpings. When Mom came in later, we didn't speak but I drank a couple glasses of her ginger ale. And then I felt so exhausted, I turned in for the night.

And the dream began again.

My breathing was hard and fast already, the sound of my exhale blocking out all other noises. *Hawh, hawh,*

hawh. My legs moved beneath me, as fast as I could make them go, faster even, they were out of control. A separate part of me, an engine churning. I had to get there, I had to get there. Where? My feet seemed to know, even though I didn't. Now my heart was pumping the blood into my ears so hard that I couldn't hear my breathing anymore. The urgent *whoosh, whoosh* blocked it out. The tombstones blurred in my vision. I have to stop him, I have to. Who? That didn't seem important. Only that I needed to run faster than it was possible. *If only, if only.* I remembered Sasha's lament. Now it was mine too. Ahead loomed the gatehouse. Was that where I was going?

I woke up with a start. Light poured in through my blinds and a million birds chirped and trilled, insisting I get out of bed. Something important needed to be done today. Monday. I had to remember to feed Misha; today was the day Mrs. Dobroski went into the hospital. But that wasn't it.

Today was the day I would call Mr. Hendricks. That was it! Maybe today I would get some answers. I dressed quickly and headed downstairs for breakfast.

Even though it was only eight o'clock by my watch, Mom was already sitting at the table eating.

"You feeling better?" she asked me.

"I think so. What's the occasion?" I noticed she wasn't sporting her usual jean and T-shirt combo. "You're not wearing a dress, are you?" I asked unbelieving as I peeked under the table to see a pair of stockinged legs and high-heeled shoes.

"Separates, actually." Mom smiled. "A skirt and

blouse. I have an appointment with the employment office at nine. Are you hungry?"

"Yeah! So hungry I could eat a —"

"Bagel." Mom passed me the plate and the cream cheese.

"Exactly." I spread the bagel, poured some orange juice and dug in. "You job hunting?"

"Yes. We could use the money right now and I need to get out."

I nodded as I chewed.

She studied me and frowned. "You'll be all right, won't you? You're really feeling better?"

"I'm fine, Mom."

"Well then, I'll be leaving. It may take some time to find the office and park the car. I want to be on time. Make a good impression, you know."

"Good luck. And Mom?"

"Yes, Nicholas?"

"You look nice."

"Thank you." Mom reached to check my forehead as she headed for the door, but I jerked away before she could manage it.

After breakfast, I took off for Mrs. Dobroski's house. I knocked first to see if she was still at home and stared at the door for a moment, waiting. Anyone could pull it off, the wood of the frame was so rotten. Finally, when no one came to the door, I inserted the key, unlocked and opened it. Classical music played from somewhere, soft and pleasant, the kind of thing my mother used to listen to and I used to complain about. The kind I missed now. The music distracted me for a moment.

Something bumped hard against my legs. I looked down. "Misha! Easy, girl. You can't be hungry yet." I went into the kitchen and read a note on the fridge.

Dear ~~Sasha~~ Nicholas,
I leave the radio playing for Misha. A half a can of food a day, plus you can fill her other bowl with dry food. She doesn't like it too much. Today, already, she has had her breakfast. Don't let her make you give her more. Perhaps a biscuit, the mocha you like so much too, is on the dining room table, you know where. Her box is in the bathroom, the kitty litter is under the sink. She uses it almost never. If I don't call you, I will be home on Friday. There's money in the soup tureen on the fridge to buy more food for Misha. But don't feed her too much! She can go out, if she likes. She will disappear for long times, she's an old gypsy, remember. She does always come home, don't worry. If you need me, I am at St. Luke's Hospital.
Bye Nicki

As I read it, Misha swished in and out between my legs. I couldn't believe Mrs. Dobroski just left her money out like that. She was so trusting. I headed for the dining room and opened the tin of biscuits. By now, Misha was tackling my ankles again.

"Here, now will you relax?" I gave her a mocha wafer and ate one myself. I surveyed the room the way a burglar might. What would Leech find worth his while to heist?

The chandelier captured a million tiny rainbows in

the crystal pendants that hung from it. It would weigh a ton, though, and take too long to remove. The furniture, while it looked like it might be antique, seemed to fall into the same category. The heavy white lace tablecloth might interest my mother, but likely not Leech. The radio playing the classical music was of the bargain basement variety. Mrs. Dobroski didn't have a CD player or a computer. The only thing that I thought would really interest Leech was the money in the soup tureen.

I looked around in the cupboards, found a bowl and carefully scooped all the money from the tureen into it. Now where should I hide it? Hmm. I swung open the freezer door and placed the bowl beside the icecube tray. "At least the old lady will have some cold cash when she gets home, eh, Misha?"

Murrow, she complained back at me.

"Okay, okay, let's check your bowls." She pushed at my heels as I walked back into the kitchen. "I see you've eaten all your canned food already. Well, that's it for today, girl. If you're hungry, you'll eat the dry stuff. Want to go outside?"

She followed me to the door and then hesitated, nosing around it.

"You don't have to go if you don't want to. But get out of my way now. I've got things to do." As quickly as I moved her out of the path of the door, she scooted back again. She wanted to follow me out, it seemed. I sighed. "All right, let's go then." I locked up, clicking my tongue at the rotting frame. Anxious now to make the phone call to that lawyer, I broke into a light run from the backyard through the cemetery shortcut.

As I crossed the main path, Leech stepped out from behind the Willobys' tombstone. "What's going on? Why's the cat from hell following you?"

"Huh? Misha's not —" But of course as I turned around, I realized that there she was, licking her white paws delicately. She stopped for a moment and meowed plaintively, showing her demon teeth to Leech. "I have no idea where she came from. Go home, girl. Shoo."

"Bull. Where's the old bat? On holidays or something, isn't she?" Leech grabbed some of my shirt in his fist. I didn't answer him and after sneering into my face for an extra-long moment, he released me. "Don't answer. I don't need your help anyway, Saint Nick. I don't need anyone." He shoved me and kicked at Misha but missed. Swearing, he walked away.

I continued on, climbing over my fence. At the patio door, I glanced back for Misha but she had disappeared. Inside, I picked up the phone and keyed in Hendricks' number.

"Hello. John Hendricks here. Can I help you?"

I was startled that he answered the phone himself. "Um, yes, this is Nicholas Dilon. I, that is to say, my family, bought the old Winfield Home."

There was a sigh at the other end of the line. "And you're calling about the Gresko ghost."

"Sir, you know?"

"I've heard about him from the various tenants who rented that house. What did you want to know?"

"Well, I understand there was an investigation into his death. Can you tell me the results?"

There was a long pause. "No."

"Sir?"

"There's nothing to tell. The investigation was inconclusive. No one seemed too anxious to find out who Alexander's murderer was. The boys at the Home refused to cooperate."

"Do you know when he died, Mr. Hendricks?"

"Oh, it was some time around the drowning. People generally assumed that it was a vendetta death. You know, he was killed because he was responsible for Corey's death."

"Do you think he was, sir?"

"No." Another big sigh. "I was."

15

"You were responsible?" I repeated, shocked.

"Of course. I should have been inspecting the property regularly, I should have noticed the hole in the fence. I should have erected another fence closer to the perimeter of the pool."

"Why does everyone blame Alexander then? I mean, not that I think they should have blamed you."

"I'm not sure. Alexander and Corey were friends. And people found it hard to believe that a fourteen-year-old inmate wouldn't have some sinister reason for befriending a five year old. Have you talked to the superintendent? He could tell you a lot more about Alexander than I can."

"You mean, Eric um . . ." I hesitated, trying to

remember the name I'd read in the newspaper article.

"Fallows." He filled in the blank for me.

"Does he still live around here?"

"Yes. He went away to university but now he teaches at Pearson. He lives over on Connor Boulevard, not far from Winfield. Do you know it?"

"I'll find it, sir."

"Two streets north of the graveyard. Let me just check the address in my file. Yup, here it is — 4315 Connor."

"Thank you."

"Not at all. Nicholas, I hope you find what you're looking for. I hope you can put Alexander to rest."

"Me too, sir. Me too." I slipped the receiver back into the cradle.

I headed out the door, back through the cemetery and past the gatehouse. Hearing a faint rustling and buzzing, I looked up. The wasps' nest. I shuddered and put a lot of room between myself and it as I walked by.

I passed through the graveyard gates, walked up Main Street and then turned onto Connor Boulevard. Now I could hear the droning of a lawnmower coming from a yard a few houses down. I followed the address numbers as I walked toward the man who was cutting his grass. He was movie star good-looking, tall with dark hair and tanned skin. As I came close to him, the noise of the lawnmower engine suddenly died. I saw a white flash of movement across his lawn.

"Excuse me. Was that your cat?" the man asked me. He spoke with the deep pleasant voice of a radio announcer.

"I don't have a —" Before I could finish, Misha dashed past. Where had she come from? "Um, yes, that is, I'm looking after her."

"Do you mind picking her up? I'm nervous about running her over." Now the man faced me, waiting patiently. I noticed a scar on one side of his face. A startling white line against his dark skin, it zigzagged from his forehead over one eyelid down to his lip. That eyelid sagged and the eye beneath it seemed to stare straight ahead. His other eye focused on me. He smiled apologetically. "I don't have such great peripheral vision."

"Sure, I'll pick her up." I tried to catch Misha but only ended up with a fistful of tail. She went manic then, hissing and swiping at me. Finally I grabbed her by the scruff of the neck and wrapped my free arm around her body. Misha dug her claws into my skin.

"Nice cat," the man commented, smiling.

"Thanks." I stroked Misha, hoping to get her to sheath her weapons. She purred but her claws still dug in. I looked up at the nearest house number — 4315. "Are you Mr. Fallows?" I asked the man with the scar.

"I am. You look familiar. Have I taught you?"

"No. I'm Nicholas Dilon. I live in the former Winfield Home."

"Oh."

"Sir. Could you tell me anything about Alexander Gresko? Mr. Hendricks said you knew him best."

"He did, did he?" Fallows wiped the back of his neck and sighed. "Why don't we sit down? Let's go over to the patio. Can I get you a lemonade?"

"No, thanks." I lowered Misha to the ground and she tore away as I sat down.

"What exactly would you like to know about Alexander?" Fallows asked me, scratching at the place on his cheek where the scar crossed.

"Anything. How did he happen to be at the Home?"

"Ah, he was a good kid. You know, you kind of remind me of him."

"I look like him?"

"Very much. You're the same height and coloring and you have the same cheekbones. You're not related?"

"No. My mom's Slovak, though. And I hear Alexander's family comes from that side of the world too."

"Maybe that's it. Anyway, Alexander had a hard life. His dad died in a work accident when he fell off a roof."

"Pardon me?" I felt a coldness grip my insides.

"His dad was a contractor and he was doing a roof. It was a damp day, he probably shouldn't have been working but no one could stop him."

Stop him! Dad was working on a roof today. Was he the one Alexander wanted me to stop? I shook the thought away. After all, it was a bright, sunny day. Dad wouldn't slip. Just the same, my mouth felt too dry and I couldn't say anything for a moment.

Fallows didn't seem to notice and continued his story. "He slipped and broke his neck. Died before they could get him to the hospital. Nothing was the same for Alexander after that. He had trouble in school, didn't get along with his mom." Fallows shook his head. "Later when she remarried, he couldn't get along with his stepdad either. One night he went for a ride with his buddies and they held up a convenience store. He claimed he didn't know what they'd been planning but it didn't make much difference with the judge. He was sent to Winfield for ten months."

"Was he friends with Corey Fairchild?"

Fallows covered his eyes with a hand for a moment. "It always comes to that."

"Sir?"

"Did you ever have five minutes of your life that you wanted to do over? Minutes that you regret so much you'd give anything, and I mean anything, if you could gain them back?"

I shook my head.

"You're too young yet." He dropped his hand and his eyes matched each other now with a dullness, a masked hurt.

"Does it have anything to do with your . . . scar?"

"This?" He pointed at his eye. "No. Four years ago, a student of mine knifed me at the high school." He shook his head. "Still, those aren't the five minutes I regret. I'd gladly lose the eye all over again if I could get back the minutes I'm talking about. They have to do with Alexander."

"And Corey?"

"Yes. Everyone blames Sasha for Corey's death." Now Fallows slipped into calling Alexander by his nickname. "Everyone, that is, except me. I know whose fault his drowning really was."

"Who was that, sir?"

"Me. I killed Corey."

First Hendricks now Fallows. I waited for him to continue.

He stared down at his hands as though looking at a bloodstain. "I was the one who ignored the hole Sasha made in the fence so the boy could slip in. I looked the other way when Sasha stayed out at night and swam past the regular hours. I believe in giving kids extra chances, do you understand?" He gestured with his hands. There was a pleading expression in his good eye.

"Yes, sir, I think I do."

"So I was the one who ignored the splashing that night. I could have at least checked!" He slapped his hands down on the patio table.

"You don't feel Sasha drowned Corey?"

"Never. He loved that kid, was giving him swimming lessons every night. Nine o'clock sharp." Fallows' lower lip trembled for a moment. "I found Corey, you know."

I nodded. "I read about that in the newspaper."

"You did, huh? Did you read that I picked him up from the bottom of the pool and pumped at his heart for ten minutes, trying to bring him back from the dead? I breathed in his mouth and he threw up all over me. But I didn't care. As long as he lived." Mr. Fallows shook his head, then traced a grey scratch in the patio table with his fingertips. "But he died again later that night. For good. I only went outside to check when I didn't hear any more splashing. If I'd gone out there five minutes earlier, Corey would have lived. Those are the five minutes I regret."

I waited for a bit before I spoke to him again. "Sir. Do you have any idea what happened to Alexander?"

"He disappeared that night. Something or someone must have stopped him or he would have been at that pool. I hunted for him later. The police wanted Alexander for questioning and I wanted to get to him first so he wouldn't be afraid. All I found was his wallet. Had a picture of his dad in it."

"Where did you find it?"

"Near the gatehouse. I felt sorry for him. I mean, if he was running away he should have at least had his wallet. He left everything else behind."

"What do you think happened to him?"

"Hitchhiked with the wrong person, who knows. They found his body so much later, the trail was pretty cold by then. And then no one really cared. There was no family around. But now . . ." Fallows wiped his hand across his face. "Now he wanders around in your backyard."

"So you know."

"I've heard the stories, never seen him."

"But you believe them?"

Fallows shrugged his shoulders. "Are you seeing him?" he asked in a voice that seemed hopeful. His good eye focused on me. He looked as though he wanted to believe.

"Yes."

"I wish I could help him in some way. Maybe you could tell him that for me?"

"I'll try."

"Good. Where's that cat of yours gone?" Fallows' eye moved side to side in its socket as he checked out the surrounding area. "I need to get back to my lawn."

I looked around but Misha had disappeared. "I think she's safe."

"Are you coming to Pearson in the fall?"

"Yes, sir."

"Well, maybe I'll teach you math." He pulled at the cord of his mower.

"Maybe," I answered and walked away.

A cloud covered the sun and the sky darkened suddenly. As I crossed through the graveyard, a light rain began, peaceful and cooling, but as it wet my skin I felt goosebumps rising. Why did the rain bother me?

Dad! *Stop him!* I broke into a run. As fast as my legs moved, it seemed as though the world began to turn in slow motion. Like in my dream. I ran past the gatehouse as fast as I could, my breathing harsh, my chest burning. I scrambled over the fence and dashed into the kitchen. "Mom!" I called.

"Yes. What is it?"

"Where's Dad working today?"

"At the other end of town. Why?"

"It's raining, shouldn't he be home?"

"It is? That came up suddenly. What's the problem?"

"You have to drive me there. Now!"

"Nicholas. I haven't been home five minutes. My feet are killing me."

"Please, Mom. It's important."

Mom slipped her heels back on, sighing. "All right. Let's go."

She adjusted the rearview mirror before she stuck the key in the ignition.

"Mom, could you hurry it up?"

She didn't answer, just backed up the car, squealing the tires. Mom's not an Indy 500 driver but she was trying. Only we hit every red light in the town. When we finally rolled onto the driveway of the old two-storey house, I saw two figures on the roof. Both wore jeans, plaid workshirts and baseball hats. I slammed the door of the car as I rushed up to the house.

"Nicholas, wait for me!"

I turned around for a split second to see Mom lose her footing on the wet grass. I wanted to go back and help her but something stronger pulled me back toward the house. Before I reached it, one of the figures on the roof slipped, tried to recover and then started to roll to the edge.

Did you ever have five minutes of your life you wanted to live over?

"Dad!" I yelled.

The figure grabbed onto the gutter and hung there.

"Hold on!" I shrieked. I searched around. "Hold on!"

I saw the ladder propped against the side of the house. Could I make it in time? I hauled it over, calling out, "To your left is the ladder. Can you catch a rung with your foot?"

He didn't respond, so I scrambled up the rungs and grabbed the lower half of his body. Dad felt different, slimmer maybe. Had he lost weight? I guided his feet to the rungs. "You can let go of the gutter now." For a few minutes, he continued to hold on. Just when I decided I'd have to climb up higher and pry his fingers loose, he grabbed hold of the ladder.

"That's great. I'm right behind you. Let's back down, easy does it. Here goes . . ." Rung by rung, we climbed down slowly. When I touched the ground again, I went to hug him, and heard a voice.

"Nicholas! Thank God you came by when you did!" Dad's voice — coming from high above me.

"What? Dad?" I looked up and saw him on the roof. Confused, I looked down again, at the face of the man slumped against the wall beside me. And realized I'd just rescued Dad's new roofing partner.

Dad climbed down the ladder. "Roy, this is my son, Nicholas."

"I can't tell you how pleased I am to meet you." Roy smiled at me. Same coloring, same clothes, almost the same build as Dad, but with a younger face.

"Let's call it quits for today." Dad lifted his baseball cap off his head, ran a shaking hand through his hair, then replaced the cap. "It just isn't worth taking any more chances."

"Fine with me," Roy answered.

"Are you all right, Roy?" Mom spoke for the first time from beside me. Her stockings were covered in mud and she held her shoes in her hands.

"Neck's a bit stiff, but otherwise I'm fine."

"Well, come on, Roy," Dad said. "Let's get out of the rain now. I'll drive you home. You can pick up your car tomorrow."

A million pounds shifted off of my back and I felt wobbly with relief. I'd stopped him. Maybe now Alexander could be happy. Maybe life could go back to normal.

Mom and I followed in the Tempo behind Dad's pickup. At Roy's house, a little kid in rain gear rushed up to him and threw his arms around his legs.

"That's his son," Mom told me. She put her hand on my shoulder. "I don't know why you had to see Dad in such a rush, but I'm glad you did."

"Me too." I couldn't say anything else, I still felt so shaky.

Twenty minutes later, we were almost home. "Mom, could you stop there?" I asked, pointing to Mrs. Dobroski's house.

I jumped out of the car and unlocked and opened the door for Misha. "Meow!" she complained to me, showing me her four demon teeth.

"Sorry, puss. Had a little emergency I had to take care of." I took a mocha biscuit from the tin in the dining room and gave it to her. Only then did she stop complaining. I slipped into the bathroom with Misha following close. Even though her box looked clean, I changed the litter. "Everything okay then, puss? I'll be back tomorrow." Misha didn't answer.

That afternoon, I helped Dad put up the towel rod that we figured would double as a ballet bar for Mom. A cool breeze drifted in through the patio window, Willy Nelson sang "Stardust" from the radio, Dad whistled along with Willy. I felt happier than I had in a long time and thought for sure I would sleep like a log that night.

But I was wrong.

Adrenalin suddenly surged through me. Running. I knew where I was the moment I felt my feet driving hard against the ground. The graveyard. I couldn't catch my breath, I'd been running so fast for so long. Would I make it in time? Could I? The gatehouse stood ahead of me like a beacon. Now I heard the rustling and buzzing ten times louder than this morning when I had actually walked by the wasps. *Stop him, stop him.* Not again, oh no!

16

Stop who? Next morning, that question shifted a million pounds of weight back onto my shoulders. I peered out the window between the slats of the blind. Clear and bright. Dad could work on the roof; there was no danger of him slipping today. I showered and dressed and headed downstairs.

Mom sat at the kitchen table, sipping coffee. She wore a navy blue dance leotard with jeans and she stared straight ahead at the want ads in the newspaper that was propped against a cereal box in front of her.

I grabbed a bowl from the cupboard and removed the cereal from under Mom's paper. The want ads flopped down — Mom looked up.

"Good morning. I take it the employment office didn't come up with any career changes for you."

"Well, no jobs actually. But the counselor had some interesting suggestions. What would you think if I taught dance?"

"I'd say you're the perfect teacher for it. Dance or sheet metal."

"Sheet metal, humph!" Mom's mouth puckered into a wry grin and then straightened. "I want to forget about that part of my professional life. It's one reason I'm glad the plant shut down."

"Glad? I thought you were upset when you lost your job."

"I worry about money. But if we can make this all work, Dad's business, the house, I'll be more than glad."

"Glad," I repeated to myself in shock, looking around at our wrecked kitchen. And then more softly to myself, "If."

"Nicholas. I'm going to the Brighton Dance Academy this morning before I lose my nerve. They're in need of a part-time instructor."

"Sure. Go for it, Mom."

She patted my arm. "Thank you, Nicholas. I knew I could count on your support. Speaking of which . . ." Her hand gripped my wrist for a moment. "Why did you want to see your father in such a hurry yesterday? In all the excitement, I forgot to ask."

"Nothing in particular. Just a strange feeling."

Mom's eyes seemed to search my face for more information. "Well, it's lucky for Roy that you had that feeling." She frowned for a moment and continued.

"But your father wanted me to leave the number of the house where he's working, just in case there's something important you do have to talk to him about."

I knew then that Dad must have told Mom about the break-ins.

"Thanks, Mom. If I think of something, I'll call him."

"Good. See you later." Mom locked the door behind her.

I stepped out the patio door into the backyard with my bowl of cereal, eating as I stood there. Ryan was walking toward the gatehouse and when he noticed me he waved.

"Don't forget about the party this Friday, Nicholas."

"I won't!"

I washed my dishes and, wanting to avoid seeing any more illegal gatehouse activities, headed the long way over to feed Misha. As I neared the house, I saw someone standing on Mrs. Dobroski's steps. Leech. He seemed to be studying the door. When I approached the walk, he took a newspaper from his canvas bag and tucked it into the rack underneath the mailbox.

"What are you doing here, Leech?"

"What's it look like I'm doing? I'm delivering *The Journal*, if it's anything to you." He stepped lightly down the stairs, waving. "See you around, Saint Nick."

The stupid door — he must know now how easy it would be to get past it, he could probably push it off its hinges. *Stop him.* Was I supposed to fix it? In order to stop Leech from breaking in? I unlocked it, brought in the newspaper and headed for the cat food on the counter.

Something pounced on my foot. "Aaah! Misha! What a watchcat you are! Too bad you can't bark." Misha figure-eighted between and around my legs as I opened a can of Meow Chow. I scooped out the spongy brown liver and tuna into her bowl and then leaned against the fridge waiting for her to scarf it up. It was satisfying to watch. I liked having the old gypsy cat waiting and dependent on me. I liked the way her whole body buzzed happily against my ankle when she finished.

"Are you coming out?" I asked her as I filled the water bowl. She ignored me and picked her way over to the dining room almost as though she understood not to step on the whites of the pattern. She leapt onto a chair, swishing her tail.

"You want dessert, huh?" I opened the tin and handed her a wafer. It only took her a few seconds to knock that back.

As I headed out the door, Misha pushed past my feet. I locked up again and leaned an elbow against the door. It groaned and gave a little. I'd call Dad right away and get him to help me.

When I dialed the number Mom had left on the fridge, it took a few rings to get an answer. Then I had to explain that Mr. Dilon really was there, he was the contractor on the roof.

Finally, I got Dad.

"Hi. You know how I'm looking after Mrs. Dobroski's house while she's in the hospital?"

"Yes. Your mother mentioned it."

"Well, the kids I told you about might want to break in there."

"When, what time? We can warn the police."

"I don't know, Dad. But I was hoping you would help me. The door frame and the door are really rotted and I'm nervous those kids I was talking about will break in through it."

"We can't just replace the frame and door without Mrs. Dobroski's permission, Nicholas."

"But I can't guard the house 'round the clock. Dad, we have to!"

"How about you pay her a visit and ask her?"

"All right. If she says yes, you'll do it right away?"

"When I get home, if you like. Tell her it will cost about four hundred dollars."

"Okay." I hung up and found the St. Luke's number in the phone book. Then I called to check the visiting hours, but the nurse told me that since Mrs. Dobroski was in a private room I could come anytime.

It was hot and fumy on the bus. I got off a couple of stops past the hospital, near the mall, so I could pick up some flowers. At the florist's, I chose a single red rose, remembering the vasefull in the center of Mrs. Dobroski's dining room table. On the way back to the hospital, I passed by Fairchild's Treasures. Stop him. I decided I needed to go inside.

The bell on the door jangled my arrival. I saw a tall, thin man get up from a chair behind the counter, hoist up his pants and adjust his glasses. "Don't tell me. You have a beatup old desk you want to sell me. Everyone thinks they have an antique in their house."

"Um, no, sir. Just browsing."

His nose twitched nervously and he looked me up

and down as though I was a potential shoplifter. "This isn't the mall, you know," he said quietly. He eyed the rose in my hand and leaned forward with his long arms on the counter. "Okay. What *do* you want?"

"Are you Corey Fairchild's father?"

"I'm nobody's father. Corey's dead." His words snapped with bitterness, and he closed his eyes for a moment. When he opened them again, he stared at me, his head at an angle. "Who are you?" You remind me of someone. Why are you asking about Corey anyway?"

"My name is Nicholas. Nicholas Dilon. I live in the Winfield house."

"You live in that . . . place." His C hissed. "That home for delinquents."

"It's not a group home anymore. You must know they closed it."

Fairchild kept talking as though he hadn't heard me. "My son died because of it. That house and Alexander Gresko."

"Alexander Gresko?" I repeated, pretending I didn't know anything. "Didn't he die a long time ago?"

"Ten years come Labor Day Weekend. But not soon enough, not before he killed my son."

"So Corey was your son," I confirmed shakily.

"That's who you look like. That murderer." He stepped around the counter.

I backed toward the door. "I . . . just live there," I said softly. "Besides, didn't the newspaper call it an accident?" *A bad accident.* Ellen Drake's words came back to me.

Fairchild shook his head. "He lured Corey into that pool and let him drown."

"That's not true. Alexander wouldn't do something like that."

"You're defending him. What are you, some relation?" His voice was loud and angry. "Corey knew how I felt about that house and those boys." He took a step toward me.

"They were friends, Mr. Fairchild." My hand touched the door handle now.

"I can't hear this." Mr. Fairchild's face crumpled as though he was about to cry, then it screwed up into a look of white rage. He reached for me but I ducked out the door.

"Don't come back!" I heard his voice from behind. The door slammed after me.

My heart pumped hard as I ran away. I only slowed down when I realized Fairchild wasn't following. Something bothered me about what he'd said. I thought it over as I walked back toward the hospital. He knew exactly when Alexander had died. Ten years this Labor Day.

Sometime around Corey's drowning, Mr. Fallows had told me. The investigation had been inconclusive, was what Mr. Hendricks had said. Yet Fairchild was certain.

Mr. Hendricks and Mr. Fallows both blamed themselves for Corey's death. But Fairchild only blamed Alexander. He was so sure and so angry. He looked about ready to kill me for just looking like Alexander. How would he have felt toward Alexander himself? He probably could have killed him with his bare hands.

And what about his connection with McNamara? McNamara drove his truck, made deliveries. He also stored stolen goods in his shed. For Fairchild? The law didn't mean anything to either of them.

Through the main door of the hospital, up through an old elevator, down a long corridor, finally outside Mrs. Dobroski's door, I hesitated. I didn't know this woman very well. If her family was in there visiting, they would wonder about me. I peered in.

Mrs. Dobroski sat alone, staring out toward the window. From what I could see, her view was pretty uninspiring, the wall of another wing of the hospital, and a pigeon-infested roof.

"Um, hi. Mrs. Dobroski?"

I was embarrassed by her reaction. The candles behind her eyes lit up and her leathery old face split into a grin.

"Come in, Nicki! How is Misha?"

"She's fine. I'm giving her a cookie every day." I stood there awkwardly, not knowing what to say next or even what to do with the rose in my hand. "Here," I finally said, handing it to her.

"So beautiful." She breathed in deeply above the flower. "It smells wonderful. I will hold it close to me, just for a little while, so I can enjoy it."

"How are you . . ." I hesitated, wondering if it were a good idea to even ask.

"Puh!" Mrs. Dobroski waved her free hand in the air. "I am old. This is one thing that will never change. The rest I do not wish to think about."

"Mrs. Dobroski, I would like to have your door and frame replaced. It costs a lot but —"

"Go ahead."

"It will be at least four hundred dollars."

"Take it from the shoe box underneath my bed."

"You agree, just like that?" Shoe box underneath her bed. Didn't Mrs. Dobroski know about banks?

"I told you. You are someone to be trusted, Nicholas."

"But I need to explain something to you. There are some boys in the neighborhood who want to rob you."

"Not again!" Mrs. Dobroski grabbed her chest.

"And I'm doing my best to watch your house. That's why I want my father to replace your frame and door, it's too easy to break in there."

"The window," Mrs. Dobroski murmured. Her eyes seemed to be staring at something else now, something beyond my shoulder.

"I'm sorry? I don't understand you."

"At first, when the window smashed, I thought it was the noise from the pool where Sasha lived. You know, when the boys jumped in the water, it sounded like that — loud."

"When the window smashed?" I repeated, confused.

"It was past eight o'clock, I remember. You must too. Stupid Sophie had already bong-bonged eight times," Mrs. Dobroski answered, as though I'd asked her what time it had happened. "We had a coffee. And then there was the smash. Sasha, you should have never chased them. You would still be alive today.

Corey would be alive." Mrs. Dobroski continued gazing at something behind me. I turned around, half-expecting Sasha to be standing there. Nothing.

"I'm not Sasha," I said softly. "I'm Nicholas."

"Nicholas." She grabbed my arm with her claw-like fingers. "Don't let it all happen again. Please."

I put my hand over hers. It was cold and bony, like a hand from the grave. I didn't know what to say. "I'll try not to, Mrs. Dobroski."

The claw relaxed and patted my arm. "You always were a good boy."

A nurse drifted in then. "Here, let me take that for you and put it in a vase. Is this your son, Mrs. Dobroski?"

"He's a good boy." Mrs Dobroski leaned back against her bed and shut her eyes.

"Well, I better be going now. Don't worry about anything, Mrs. Dobroski." She didn't answer me. She didn't even open her eyes.

That evening, Dad and I went to her house with the materials to fix the door. It took almost till midnight, first removing the old frame and door and then hammering up a new one.

"She won't have any problems with this one," Dad told me when the new oak door was in place.

"She's more worried about the window," I told him, thinking over what she'd talked about in the hospital. "Someone once tried to break in by smashing it." *And then Sasha chased them and McNamara caught him, and threw him against the gatehouse.* That had to be why Corey died. McNamara killed Sasha before he could get to Corey for the swimming lesson! Wasn't that what Dobroski said?

In the state she was in, who would ever believe her? She was right. No one listens to anyone who forgets your name ten seconds after you tell them.

"Nicholas, which window?" Dad asked.

"In the back, I guess."

We walked around together. Dad screwed up his mouth as he looked at it. "She wouldn't want bars on it, I'm sure, and the window does lock." Dad scrunched up his face. "The real problem is that the house backs onto the graveyard. Anyone could come up this way and probably no one would see them."

"Could we tell the police?"

"Sure, but it's too late tonight."

"Dad. One more thing." I rushed into the house with him behind me. I found Mrs. Dobroski's bedroom and reached underneath the bed. Sure enough, there was a shoe box. I opened it. "I'm supposed to pay you from this."

Dad whistled softly. "That's a pile of money. How much is in there?"

I counted the bills out loud. There were three thousand and twenty dollars, not including Dad's four hundred. "Dad, can we put this in the bank for her?"

"I think we better. She obviously doesn't like banks but since there's a danger of burglary . . ." Dad reached out his arm and I handed him the shoe box.

"Wait, there's more in the freezer." I went to the kitchen and took out the soup tureen money. Then we returned home in the pickup.

I was so tired I didn't even bother to change my clothes. I fell across my bed and slept.

A crash and the tinkling of shards called to me from somewhere. Was it a window shattering? Almost immediately, I was running again. Chasing and escaping endlessly. Powered by a strong energy that crackled through me like lightning, I felt the vibrations of my feet as they hit the ground. My heart knocked against my chest with every step. Faster, faster, *hawh, hawh, hawh*, my breathing became loud and hard. Where was I running to? Now I could see the tombstones as I flew by them, a grey and white blur, now I was approaching the gatehouse, stark and silent in the moonlight. Now I could hear the rustling and buzzing of the wasps' nest. And now a shadow loomed up ahead. McNamara leapt out at me.

17

"Do you know how long the owner will be away?" From behind her desk, Officer Vellenga's green eyes stared at me unblinking. Her golden brown hair was tucked away at the back of her head. That and those eyes made me think of Shannon.

"I'm sorry." I forced myself to concentrate. "Mrs. Dobroski's in for tests at the hospital till Friday."

Dad leaned forward in his chair. "The problem is my son knows that some teenagers in our neighborhood are planning to break into her house." He glanced at his watch. We'd already deposited Mrs. Dobroski's money but Dad had to meet Roy at ten o'clock to finish the roofing job.

"Well, I *think* they're planning to," I piped in. I

wanted everything to be down on paper exactly correct. This was the easy part, after all, not the ghost floating in the backyard warning me, just the hard facts. "He makes threats."

"Who is 'he' and what kinds of threats?" She gripped her pen tightly.

I frowned. "His nickname is Leech. I don't know his other names. He just kind of shoves me around. Wants to know what Mrs. Dobroski has in her house. Wants me to help him." I pictured Officer Vellenga asking me to wear a wire to record Leech's threats, like people did on television.

Instead, she nodded and added some notes to her file. "Do you know where he lives?"

"No." I chewed the inside of my mouth as I thought.

"What are you going to do, Officer?" my father asked.

"Well, we can take down a description of Leech, find and question him, maybe put some fear into him."

"But then he'll know I told you." I rubbed the fading bruises on my elbow.

Officer Vellenga nodded, frowning. "It does put you in some danger. Especially if Leech doesn't scare easily."

"What's the alternative?" Dad asked.

"We can put Mrs. Dobroski's house on a special attention list so the officers assigned to that area will make a point of driving by during their patrol. You say she gets home from the hospital on Friday?"

"Yes."

"A police cruiser will pass by the house as often as possible. That usually acts as a deterrent. We could even get lucky and catch Leech in the act. Here, take my number, Nicholas." She handed me her business card. "If you hear anything else, something more specific, you can call me." Officer Vellenga stared straight into my eyes, waiting. It was as though she knew I wasn't telling her everything.

Stop him. If I told her about McNamara's involvement, would Jeff and Ryan lose their father? I heard Jeff crying in my mind. Marian's mother had treated Jeff for a broken arm. But had McNamara really caused it?

I had no choice, I decided. "I think . . ." I cleared my throat, "that is, I've seen Leech take stolen goods into the Winfield cemetery gatehouse."

"Ah. This is a new development. You're sure these goods are stolen?" she asked.

I shrugged my shoulders. "Pretty sure. He brings them in a newspaper cart or bag and McNamara, he's the caretaker, gives him money."

"Hmm. We'd need a search warrant."

"But McNamara takes the stuff out all the time."

"So we'd have to be lucky to catch him with anything." She frowned.

"He makes deliveries for Fairchild's Treasures. You know — the antique shop."

"I know Fairchild well."

"Maybe you could find some stolen goods at the store. I think that he's involved."

"Again, we'd have to be pretty lucky. Fairchild's a real antique nut but he's not stupid. He'd never keep anything in the store unless it was so old he couldn't part with it. Is there anything else?"

I did want to tell her more. *There's a ghost who visits our backyard. I think he's trying to tell me who murdered him. I dream about it every night.* Was that even what I was really dreaming about? I wasn't sure. In any case, she wouldn't believe me, she wouldn't take down any more notes after that.

She watched me for another moment. Then she reached out to shake Dad's hand. "Thank you very much for coming in, Mr. Dilon. We'll keep an eye on Mrs. Dobroski's house, as I said." Now she reached out to shake my hand. "If anything else comes up, you have my card." She had a strong grip and again I thought of Shannon. "Nicholas, if you hear or see anything more . . ." She didn't finish.

I could just imagine calling her up and trying to explain Sasha.

"Thanks again." Officer Vellenga stood up. She wasn't as tall as Shannon.

On the way home, Dad dropped me off at Mrs. Dobroski's so I could give Misha her daily tuna and liver mush. I'd just started the can opener when something rattled at the front door.

Misha's tail stood up and waved ominously.

"What's that, puss?" I asked her.

She tiptoed toward the door. This time someone pounded. Leech? Maybe he'd found out about our trip to the police station.

I grabbed the first knife I saw from the cutlery

drawer and hesitated, still hoping whoever it was would go away.

The door rattled again and I was glad Dad had replaced the old rotting one. I stepped through the hall, unlatched the chain and twisted the knob quickly, yanking back at the same time.

A short person fell against me. I dropped my weapon which turned out to be a butter knife, and caught his arm. "Jeff! What are you doing here?"

He scrambled up. "You're never at the pool anymore. I wanted to talk to you." Jeff wiped his hand across his face, leaving a grey smudge on his cheek.

"That's true. I've been busy."

"They close the pool this weekend."

Labor Day. It made sense.

He folded his arms across his chest. "You said you'd teach me to swim." He looked at me, eyes narrowing, accusing.

I shrugged.

"C'mon, Nicholas, you promised!" Now he was pleading.

"All right already, Jeff. How about this afternoon?"

"Sure!" His arms dropped down and a smile brightened his face.

If only someone could solve my problems so easily. I returned to the can opener.

"Can I feed the kitty?" Jeff asked when he saw me reach for the can.

"You shouldn't even be in here. This isn't my house." I watched Jeff's smile droop. "But I guess it can't hurt. Here you go." I handed him the spoon and the mush. We watched together as Misha enjoyed her breakfast and gave herself a bath.

"Now dessert," I told Jeff, handing him my mocha biscuit and dropping one for Misha. In seconds they were both finished. "All set? Let's go."

Misha swished past my ankles. It was too early for the pool, but Jeff walked alongside of me, showing no signs of going home. "I haven't had breakfast so I'm going home to make myself some Pizza Pops," I told him.

"Can I have some too?"

"I guess." He followed me into the house. "Wait here," I told him as I slid a plate full of pizza into the microwave. Then I headed upstairs to collect my bathing suit and two towels. Jeff had already removed the plate by the time I returned and was tearing into the pizza.

"Ow, ow, hot!" he yelped, showing me an open mouthful of sauce and cheese.

"You're supposed to let it sit for a minute." I got him a glass of water. "Here, take a swallow. What's the matter, doesn't your mother ever feed you?" I'd forgotten what his answer would be.

"Uh uh," he answered, gulping. "My mother doesn't live with us." Jeff told me this with no sadness in his voice, but his eyes looked hesitant as though expecting some kind of judgement or rejection.

I didn't say anything.

"Can we play Nintendo after?" His eyes brightened with hope.

"I don't have Nintendo. But we can play computer games."

"All right!" Jeff shouted enthusiastically. In record time, he finished his lunch. "Can we play now?"

"Wait till I'm finished."

Jeff bounced in his chair as I ate. I went to grab his T-shirt to make him hold still but he winced and ducked away as though expecting me to hit him. In the same moment, I felt sorry and shocked. "Go wash your hands before you touch the computer," I told him finally.

Zip, zap and he followed me into Mom's office. Pounding on her stapler, he had it jammed in minutes. "How do you turn the computer on?" His fingers were already pushing and prodding at every key and button.

Again, I wanted to grab him and hold his arms and hands still. Then I pictured him wincing and ducking. I remembered the scream I'd heard coming from his house and the tears when I knocked on the door. I could imagine McNamara's fist crashing into Jeff's small body and so I took a deep breath. "Let me, Jeff."

He's only a baby, I kept reminding myself whenever Jeff bugged me. Although I was angry with McNamara, I wondered just how easy it might be to slip into the habit of knocking a kid around. I was happy when it came time to go to the pool and even happier when Marian agreed to go with us.

Skipping along beside us, Jeff seemed like just another happy-go-lucky kid. He peeled off his outer shorts and scrambled into the pool the moment we got there.

We'd hardly been in the water when a purple bruise of a cloud blocked the sun.

"Oh, oh, looks like it might rain," Marian commented.

"We don't care," Jeff yelled and tugged on my arm. "Come on. Show me how, Nicholas."

The sky rumbled. For a moment I thought a plane was flying overhead.

"What was that?" Marian asked. No one had time to answer her. The same musclebound lifeguard who'd escorted me out last week blew twice into his whistle, long and hard. Shannon's voice came to us over a bullhorn.

"Would everyone please leave the pool, lightning has been spotted."

"Aw, man!" Jeff complained. "She always makes us wait half an hour before we can go back in."

The sky darkened even more and a pitchfork of lightning shot down.

"Forget it, Jeff. Might as well head home."

"But I need to be able to swim for Friday."

"Why?"

"The guys always go swimming. Ryan, Leech. The whole gang. Every year they break into the pool after sundown to have their last swim of the summer."

"And they take you?"

He stared down at his toes. "No."

"Well then, since you're not going anyway, what's the problem? Besides, we can swim tomorrow."

"I can't," Marian told us. "My mother's taking me shopping for school clothes."

"Don't you just hate it? I'm going Friday," I complained. Jeff's mouth sunk. "So that's still okay. Marian and I can take turns. I'll teach you Thursday. Marian can do it Friday."

"That would be great! Do you think I can learn in two days?"

"Sure," I lied. What harm could encouraging the kid do? "Right now, let's get you home, before it starts to pour."

The rain pattered down on us as we made it to McNamara's house. I'd saved Jeff a morning of boredom or worse, but in the end I needed to let him go back to it. The sky opened up but we didn't even hang around underneath the porch. Marian and I were both drenched when we dashed down our separate paths. I took the steps up the porch two at a time and from the door the sound of Dad's whistling called me to the kitchen.

"Hi, Dad!" I called.

He waved and opened his lips a little so I would see the screws he was holding between his teeth.

"I'm just going to go dry off." I pointed upstairs.

Dad nodded, dropping a couple of screws.

I changed my clothes and then opened the slats of my blinds. Ryan stood at the door of the gatehouse in the downpour. It was only the second time I'd seen him there. The door opened and he disappeared inside.

We're not allowed in there, Jeff had said. And then something else he'd said came to my mind. *My brother saw a body in there once when he was my age.* What other body could it have been but Sasha's? *My age, my age.* Ryan would have been around Jeff's age when Sasha had been killed. *And then Sasha chased them and McNamara caught him, and threw him against the gatehouse.* Mrs. Dobroski's words. Mr. Fallows had found Sasha's wallet near the gatehouse. It all made sense. I thought of calling Officer Vellenga. Except it had all happened a long time ago and what real proof did I have? Sasha appearing at the pool at night talking his misery through my lips, that was what really convinced me. I didn't think it would work for anyone else, especially not someone like Officer Vellenga. I could picture her tossing back her hair and laughing and then I realized it was really Shannon in the picture.

Lying in my bed that night, I was afraid to close my eyes even though it felt as though tombstones weighted them down. What was the point? I'd only start up on that awful treadmill, running, running, never quite escaping, never quite making it in time. For what?

I closed my eyes for a moment, willing myself not to sleep. And then I smelled it. That heavy, choking chlorine smell. I wanted to get up and go to the window. Sasha must be there. Maybe he would tell me something. But suddenly I wasn't in bed anymore. I was standing on a diving board, bouncing slightly. The sky burned bright orange and yellow with the last traces of a sunset. I heard a loud, hard splash, the sound of a cannonball dive, or was it glass shattering? I couldn't be sure. I leapt up, up, up, straight and high in the air and then I turned, arrowing my body down into the water. Like a sword I stabbed through, white bubbles rushing past me. For a moment it felt like a good dream.

And then the pain clutched at my stomach. I resisted doubling up, instead swimming frantically around. Where is he? Where is he? My eyes and throat burned as though I'd swallowed the sun. Now everything became dark and I pulled hard toward the surface. I needed to breathe. One last final thrust into the air. And then lightning cracked through the darkness, lighting up my nightmare.

I heard the shattering and splintering of a thousand pieces of glass. Now I was running. Away from Dobroski's house, into the graveyard. Hurry, hurry, hurry, my breath rushed out and out and out. There never seemed a moment to inhale. My heart crashed into my throat over and over. I heard it shattering and splintering. I was dying. I couldn't run faster, and I wasn't going to make it in time. All the graves were covered in roses. I smelled their cloying sweetness. They waved to me, lie down, lie down, rest, rest. I kept running.

The gatehouse rose up in front of me, like a stone mountain. I heard rustling and buzzing. I saw McNamara, his face misshapen with anger. His arm reached out and I couldn't make my legs move fast enough. His fingers were inches from my throat. Another doubled-up fist flew toward my face. Again I heard a hard splash, a cannonball dive or a window shattering. Lightning flashed through the sky. And then there was an ear-piercing scream. *Stop him!*

18

I woke up still screaming. The brightness of my bedroom told me it was already morning.

Mom rushed into the room. "Nicholas! What's wrong?" She sat down on the edge of the bed. "Bad dream?"

"It was so real." I held my head with my hands.

"Do you want to tell me about it?" She brushed back the hair from my forehead.

"No!" I jerked away from her. She wouldn't want to hear it anyway.

"Fine, Nicholas," she said with a heavy tiredness.

"I just don't want to think about it anymore," I told her more calmly.

"Well, get dressed and come downstairs. You'll forget all about it soon." She left my bedroom.

No. I'd never forget about it. That might be Mom's method, pushing everything aside, pretending it would go away. But Sasha would never let me forget. I lay back and shut my eyes. McNamara's fist came for me again in my mind. I forced my eyes open before it connected.

A loud rushing noise came from the open window. I walked over there, and felt the rain sprinkling my face. And Jeff wanted to go swimming. Too bad. The kid seemed to know too much about disappointment already. I shut the window, and my mind, to his problems.

McNamara's fist — even with my eyes open, loomed over me. Who could tell me what had really happened to Sasha? It wasn't something McNamara would be happy to chat about. *Stop him.* I had to do something.

Mrs. Dobroski — I would go to her. This time I would make her tell me everything. She had to know more. "Could you drop me off at the hospital? I want to visit Mrs. Dobroski," I called when I noticed Mom heading for the door.

"Sure. Grab your jacket. Let's go."

The wipers fought the downpour off the windshield as the Tempo crawled through the storm toward St. Luke's. I ducked my head as I dashed from the car to the hospital entrance, giving Mom a wave before she headed off.

This time I knew where I was going and I didn't

hesitate outside Mrs. Dobroski's door. I knocked softly and continued in.

She was facing the window but her eyes didn't seem to be focused on the brick wall and roof view. Where was her mind today?

"Mrs. Dobroski?" I called softly.

Her face broke open with a happy smile. "Sasha, you're back."

"I'm not Sasha." I needed to keep her in this world. "Mrs. Dobroski, it's me, Nicholas."

Her smile melted and then her eyes brightened as she focused on me. "Of course. Nicki, so good to see you!"

"It's nice to see you too. Are you . . . okay?"

"I am fine, Nicholas, just fine now." Her smile spread across her face once again.

"I need to talk to you about Sasha. I need to know exactly what happened that last night you saw him."

Mrs. Dobroski's head shook slightly. It was almost a tremor.

"It's important. I think I'm seeing Sasha. I think he's warning me about something in my dreams."

"Sasha?" she repeated in a faraway voice as she turned to look out the window.

"Mrs. Dobroski, please," I begged, grabbing her bony hands in my own. "You said he never should have chased them. Remember the window was smashed, and Sasha ran?"

"The window was smashed," Mrs. Dobroski repeated as though in a trance. "And you ran outside." Her voice became steady and the words came quicker. "There were two big boys. 'Leave them!' I called to you but you would not listen. You chased them. And I heard you shouting at them. You were not going to let them get away with this. You knew everything, about McNamara, Fairchild." Now Mrs. Dobroski's head was shaking. "What did it matter about a silly smashed window? Why did you have to chase them?"

"Mrs. Dobroski, go on." I squeezed her hand.

"But you ran and I came after you. I came to the gatehouse and saw McNamara." Mrs. Dobroski's breathing became loud and raspy. "He hit out at you and you fell against the wall. Oh, Sasha! That terrible noise. When your head hit that wall, you didn't cry out, but it was like a rock hitting against another rock. Your body seemed empty after that moment. And then he threw you into the gatehouse. 'Good riddance to bad rubbish,' he said as he did this terrible thing."

"That's why Sasha never made it to Corey's swimming lesson," I mused out loud.

"Nobody saw me in the darkness. Only Misha. Misha, who cried so terribly when her tail was broken. I picked her up and ran home."

"And you didn't tell the police."

"The police! Pah! When I was a little girl, they took my father away in the middle of the night and I never saw him again."

"The police aren't like that here," I told her.

"Do not believe that. What is an old woman to them when they have big-shot Harold Fairchild telling them that Alexander Gresko is a criminal?"

"But, Mrs. Dobroski, I have to go to the police."

"No, Sasha, don't do it. They'll go after you again."

Mrs. Dobroski grabbed at my jacket, trying to hold me there.

"Listen to me," I told her firmly. "It's different here. I know a police officer, Officer Vellenga, you can trust her."

Mrs. Dobroski stared out the window again. "You have to help me." I shook her till she focused back inside. "I need to stop McNamara. Sasha wants me to."

Tears filmed her eyes then. Her lip trembled and she touched my face with her hand. "God be with you, Nicholas."

I gently took her hand away from my face. "Don't worry, Mrs. Dobroski. He is." I laid her hand down on the bed and patted it. "See you soon."

From the hospital, I walked directly to the police station. The rain continued, slicking my hair to my face and making my clothes heavy and uncomfortable.

Officer Vellenga didn't seem surprised to see me. "Nicholas, I'm glad you decided to come back."

"This isn't exactly about the break-in."

"Whatever you want to talk to me about —" She threw up her hands. "I'll listen." She motioned me to the chair opposite her.

I started with what Ryan and Leech had said in front of Fairchild's Treasures.

Officer Vellenga nodded. "There have been rumors about Fairchild. But he's pretty active in community charity and such. And no one's been able to catch him with any stolen merchandise."

Encouraged, I told her about McNamara beating Jeff.

"Nicholas, you didn't witness the beating, did you?" She leaned back in her chair as if distancing herself from her notes.

"No, but I heard Jeff screaming."

Vellenga bit at her lip and sat forward again. "Okay." She wrote something down.

Then I took a deep breath. I told her about what Mrs. Dobroski saw and about Eric Fallows finding Alexander Gresko's wallet.

"Yes, Nicholas, is there something more?"

I stopped and I stared into her green eyes, trying to measure their belief in me. "Well yes, there's this ghost and I have these strange dreams . . ." I let the whole story loose on her and waited for a response.

Officer Vellenga tapped the end of her pen on the desk and frowned.

"You don't believe anything I said, do you?" I asked.

She leaned back again. "Look, Nicholas, last year when a child disappeared, we checked near a lake because her mother dreamed she saw her there."

"Did you find the kid?"

"Yes. But it was too late, she had died of hypothermia."

Everything went cold inside me. "I don't know what else to do. I don't know anybody else to turn to. I just know I have to stop him."

"It's all right, Nicholas. I'll take down the facts. Those are the only things that will hold up in a court of law. But on that other stuff, I keep an open mind."

"But you can't do anything about it."

"Nicholas." Now she sat forward and gripped the sides of her desk. "I'm the one who went to the lake for that little girl." Her eyes looked directly into mine.

I nodded, feeling somewhat stronger because of her story. I reached out to shake her hand and she held it for an extra moment as she continued. "I'll see what I can do with what you've given me. Who knows what we'll turn up."

"Thanks," I told her.

"The extra patrol is still in effect till tomorrow. And I'll talk to Mrs. Dobroski."

"She's nervous about police."

Officer Vellenga smiled. "I'll go off duty, no uniform. Thank you, Nicholas."

The rain continued the rest of the day and into the night. The sound of water drip-dripping into the house drove Mom and me crazy till we found it leaking from a basement window and set up a bucket there. Dad came home and immediately worked on plugging the leak. There was no time to think of anything else.

Bedtime came and went and I paced my room. I watched the graveyard, watched the trees waving, and the raindrops hitting the puddles near the headstones, making tiny ripples. Finally I lay down.

From somewhere faraway yet deep inside my head, I heard a thunk and felt warm liquid dripping from my ears. I was suspended in water, beautiful, aquamarine. I felt warm all over. My heart beat very slowly, very loudly. I heard it echo from all around me.

Floating, floating, there was a problem I was supposed to look after but it seemed to float away along with the panic and urgency I had felt running through the graveyard the night before. The sweet smell of roses called to me. Relax, slow down, float.

My heart beat even slower. Thump, thump, thump, thump and then I didn't hear it anymore. I don't know how long I floated like that before I smelled a different, more disturbing smell. Chlorine. I sat up, wide awake now, but the smell didn't go away. Instead it grew stronger, biting at my nostrils and the back of my throat.

"Sasha, you're here." At the end of the bed he stood, his body and face clearer than they'd ever been. His hair was dark, almost black, his eyes soft brown and he had high cheekbones. He reminded me of someone but at first I couldn't figure out who. Then it hit me, as it must have everyone else who knew him. Sasha looked like me.

Sasha stared at me, not speaking, but I could feel his sorrow, his regret. My body echoed his heaviness.

"How can I stop him?" I asked. I felt tears on my face and I was sobbing but Sasha still stared. "You have to help me," I begged.

Sasha nodded. "It's time," he told me in my own voice. And then his presence faded so quickly I wasn't sure anymore if he hadn't been just another part of the dream.

19

"Nicholas, you promised!"

Friday morning, and I knew from the moment I opened my eyes, that it was time. I kept thinking of Sasha at the end of my bed. Time for something important, something that would change all other things, and I had a pretty clear feeling it wasn't back-to-school shopping. "Mom, there's something important I have to do."

"What?" Mom planted her hands on her hips.

"I have to feed Misha, I have a party to go to tonight, I should probably go to the pool this afternoon." I was desperately rhyming off things but she didn't take her hands off her hips.

"You can feed the cat on the way out and you

aren't going to any party unless you hold to our agreement about shopping."

"But I don't need new clothes."

"You can't wear cutoffs to school, I'm sorry! Three pairs of jeans, two shirts and a pair of shoes, I won't settle for anything less. The sooner we get there, the sooner you're done."

I knew I had to give in but I couldn't switch off that feeling. Something important was about to happen. It was time. And now maybe I'd be away at the critical moment.

The telephone rang as Mom shut the door behind us.

"We'll let the answering machine get it. It's probably just someone wanting to vacuum our ducts."

I stared back at the house as we pulled out of the driveway. I hate not answering the phone. I always imagine that we're missing some crucial piece of information when we ignore it, someone needing our help, someone letting us know we've won a contest (but only if we're at home to receive the call), someone dying.

When we stopped at Mrs. Dobroski's, I finally blocked out the ringing phone, changed the litter box and fed Misha as quickly as I could. Afterward she padded into the dining room expectantly. Instead of following her, I snuck out the front. "Mommy's coming home today, don't worry, you'll get your cookie," I called back. I wanted Misha to be waiting for Mrs. Dobroski when she returned, not prowling the graveyard.

We arrived at the mall and Mom and I disagreed over everything. Finally, in the Patches Boutique when she saw the price tags, she told me to go ahead and choose something on my own. "I'll put thirty dollars toward each item of clothing I mentioned. You spend whatever you like as long as you pay the balance."

At that moment, a tall girl drifted into the store. Shannon. It was too much to think about all at the same time. Mom handed me some money. "We'll meet at the water fountain at two."

I nodded and just in time, Mom left. "Hi, Shannon." She was close enough to touch now.

"Hi, Nick." She fingered a pair of the soft blue jeans and eyed the tag.

"You going to the party tonight?" I asked.

"Yeah, it's kind of a tradition. I just hope those idiots don't break into our pool."

"That's a tradition too, I hear."

"Yeah, but it's a dumb one. They drink and get stupid. It's too dangerous." Shannon looked at a red and blue Looney Tunes tie. "Don't you just love these?"

"Yeah. Why doesn't someone just stop them?" I asked. *Stop him.* Was this the mission Sasha wanted to send me on?

"People always try. The cops come some years. But accidents happen. The idea of kids in our pool after hours makes me nervous."

Pool accidents — it made me edgy and uncomfortable too. But over the last couple of weeks, everything made me feel that way. I casually moved over to the shirts, hoping she would follow.

"That would go great with the tie," Shannon commented over the one I was eyeing.

"You think so?"

"Uh huh. See you tonight, Nick." Shannon smiled.

Her smile almost made me forget my uneasiness. Mom hadn't said anything about a tie but I bought it and the shirt. I picked up the soft jeans but because I paid ninety dollars for them, I bought my sneakers at a bargain table. My mouth turned really dry after that so I headed for a stand in the food court. I passed an antique display in the center of the mall, but didn't think anything of it till I saw Fairchild standing ahead of me in line. And in front of him, McNamara.

"You following me or something?" Fairchild tugged at his pants as though it proved something.

"No," I answered flatly and then continued staring at him.

"Does this kid look familiar to you?" he asked McNamara.

McNamara stepped closer to me, squinting and frowning. "Yeah. He took Jeff swimming the other day. Why?"

"He doesn't remind you of anybody?" Fairchild's eyebrows stretched up. His eyes grilled McNamara.

"Nah, he's a young punk, same as all the others. Why should he?"

"He's been poking around. I think he's related to the delinquent that killed Corey."

"Alexander never killed Corey!" I snapped before thinking.

McNamara's hands bunched into fists.

In a quick flash from my nightmare, I saw him lash out at me. "*You* did!" I blurted out, pointing my finger at him.

Now his face mottled over with red and white splotches and he sputtered, "Why, you lying son of a —" He never finished. Instead he reached out to grab me but I tore off into the crowd.

Just when I thought I'd put a safe distance between us, a hand caught me by the shoulder. I pulled away and whirled around with my elbows out as battering rams.

"Nicholas! What's the matter?" Mom stepped back.

"Oh, it's you." My arms relaxed back down at my sides. "Nothing, Mom, just jumpy I guess."

"Well, take a deep breath. How did you manage?"

My hands shook as I offered up my bags for her inspection. She didn't seem to notice. "Pricey jeans," she commented as she checked out the tags. "Two more pairs to go. There's a sale on at Sears. C'mon, you had your chance to shop alone."

Sears, the other side of the mall. I tried to lose myself as we walked along. I kept my face to the store windows and ducked behind others just in case McNamara was out there somewhere. Why did I have to go and tell him what I thought about Sasha's murder? Warn him was what I'd just done. Another part of my nightmare came back to me — the running, the hard breathing, my heartbeat, the stone gatehouse and the end — McNamara leaping out and shooting his fist at me.

"What about these?"

Now we were in the youth department of Sears. "What? Oh. They're okay, Mom," I told her shakily. I reached out with sweaty hands and Mom piled them full with black jeans, a sweatshirt and a pair of grey track pants. I'd never been such an agreeable shopper, trying them all on, mumbling, "They're great." Finally, we finished.

"Should we grab some lunch at the food court?"

"Can we just go home instead?" What if McNamara and Fairchild were still there?

"I guess so. Might as well save some money and eat back at the house."

I tried to put some purpose and speed into our walk back toward the door, but Mom resisted, ambling up to clothes racks and shuffling through the dresses.

"Can we go?" I asked her with a little more force.

"Nicholas, you're rushing me! I think it's time you learned some patience."

It's time. His words. Sasha standing at the foot of my bed. *Stop him.* Whatever was going to happen was going to happen soon. "Mom, can't you browse the mall without me?"

"Right, Nicholas." Her face set into a tombstone. She strode ahead, forcing me to sprint to catch up.

Through the passageway, out the door, slamming the car door, she didn't say a word to me. When we were a few blocks away from the house the weather turned strange.

"What the —" The sun still filled the sky with a hot white brightness, but hail hammered at the car.

Up ahead there was a tall figure running, almost stumbling, hands over her head to protect herself from the hard pellets. Mom pulled up ahead of her near the curb. "Marian!" she called. "Get in! We'll give you a lift."

Marian slid into the backseat, breathless and wet. "Have you seen Jeff?" she asked me.

"No, why?"

"It was my turn to give him his swimming lesson, remember? I went to his house and no one answered so I went to the pool to see if he was there."

"And?"

"Not there. I thought maybe he'd gone to your house and that's where I was heading."

"He's probably somewhere with Ryan and Leech," I answered. "There was a phone call the answering machine picked up just as we were leaving."

"You think he'd call you?" Marian brightened just as I realized he probably couldn't, not knowing my phone number.

I shrugged. "You never know with Jeff." And that was certainly true. He had found me at Mrs. Dobroski's the other day.

Marian seemed satisfied that Jeff was taken care of now. "Are you going to the Youth Bonfire this evening?"

"Youth Bonfire?" I repeated. Bonfire had a different ring to it than bush party, not like something Ryan and Leech would attend. "I don't know."

"Hey, I thought you were planning on it," Mom said. "Go on and meet some more people."

"My mother can drive us."

Was that where Sasha wanted me to be? If only I knew what it was time for. Shannon would be there. In the end, that detail swayed me. "Yeah, I'll go."

"I'm bringing a cooler of soft drinks and marsh-mallows."

"I'll bring some chips."

"Great," Marian said. Mom stopped our car in her driveway and Marian jumped out. "Come over to my house at around eight." Then she hesitated. "Let me know about Jeff, okay?"

"Anything I find out, you'll know," I promised her.

"There won't be any drinking at this bonfire, will there?" Mom asked as we drove up to our house.

Where was Jeff? I asked myself as we got out and headed in the front.

"You're not answering me, Nicholas."

"Well, you heard Marian. She's bringing soft drinks."

"You know what I mean."

Her tone annoyed me. Why couldn't she stick her head in the sand about stuff like school clothes and bush parties? She could do it okay with the house and the neighborhood. "Mom, I will be drinking soft drinks. If someone brings a case of beer, don't worry, I won't drink any."

"Good."

We walked into the house.

Mom pressed a button on the answering machine to listen to our messages. I wondered about Jeff. Should I look up McNamara's number and check on him?

"I'll be home at five o'clock today. See you then." Dad's recorded voice, click, and then the answering machine continued.

"This is a message for Nicholas Dilon from Nurse Christine Sallie, intensive care at St. Luke's Hospital. Would you give me a call at 555-0688? Thank you."

Mom looked at me.

Forgetting about Jeff now, I rushed to the phone and dialed the number.

"Hello, Nicholas. I'm glad you called," Nurse Sallie said when I identified myself. "This isn't the best news and I'm not sure how close you are to her."

My mouth suddenly turned dry. "She's not . . ."

"Dead? No, no. But I'm afraid she's experiencing some cardiac problems. Yesterday afternoon she had a mild heart attack."

I was there yesterday.

"Listen, the reason I called specifically is that Mrs. Dobroski seemed very concerned about her cat. You're looking after her?"

"Yes. Tell her not to worry. I'll take care of Misha till she gets back."

"I'm sure she'll feel much better knowing that. Nicholas, she's disoriented and upset right now. She made me promise to give you a message."

"She did? What was it?"

"Don't bother about the window and don't follow them. Does that mean anything to you?"

Mrs. Dobroski was confusing me with Sasha again. I sighed. "Yes."

"Good. Her daughter will be flying in so she may contact you later. Thank you for calling, Nicholas."

"You're welcome." I laid the receiver back down on the counter.

"Bad news?" Mom asked.

"Yeah. Mrs. Dobroski's had a heart attack."

Mom touched my shoulder. I only realized in that

instant how badly I felt. Mrs. Dobroski had been so excited when I'd made her talk about Sasha. Had I caused this?

"She's in the best place in the world for it, at least." Mom smiled at me.

"But she's so old."

"Try not to think about it, Nicholas." Mom's standard answer to dealing with uncomfortable situations. She hugged me then. "It just doesn't help."

Dad came home early, as he'd promised, and we ate supper together. I couldn't stop staring out the window as I chewed on some meat — beef, I think. No more hail now but the air was hot, stifling, and heavy with pre-storm humidity. I noticed McNamara puttering around the gatehouse and I shifted uncomfortably in my chair, thinking about Jeff.

"Eat your broccoli, Nicholas," Mom instructed, glancing my way.

"I hate —" I started but then realized I'd eaten almost all of it anyway without even noticing.

After supper, I took a long cool shower. Then I threw on my new blue jeans. I thought about wearing my shirt and tie but decided it was too hot and way too obvious a move for Shannon's attention. A tie to a bush party! I laughed out loud. When I passed near the clothes hamper, I noticed Mrs. Dobroski's key on the floor where it must have dropped from my dirty clothes. For a fleeting second I thought I smelled chlorine. It must be coming from my wet bathing suit in the hamper, I decided as I scooped up the key and shoved it in my pocket.

Jeff — was there time to check on him now? I headed back to my room and looked through my blinds over the graveyard toward his house. All the windows were dark. Would he be asleep already? Nah, he must have gone to visit someone.

I combed my hair, splashed on some aftershave and spent another fifteen minutes pacing in front of my window.

Finally it was time to go so I grabbed a bag of chips from the pantry and headed for Marian's. As I stepped outside, for a moment I smelled the chlorine again, but when I took a deep breath it was gone.

"You have the cooler in the trunk?" Dr. James asked Marian as we sat in the car. "Did you take a sweater in case it gets cold?" Marian nodded to all the questions. "All right then, let's go."

We drove down Main Street in the opposite direction of the mall and swung off after a couple of minutes. "There's the park, you can see it in the distance over there," Marian pointed.

The sun burned a fiery hole over the hill toward where she pointed. We drove another five minutes and then stopped at the brown and yellow park gate. A ranger smiled and waved us through.

"A park this close to home. At least there's some advantage to living in the boonies," I said, half-kidding.

Dr. James looked at me coldly and then turned her attention to winding the car up the hill. At the top, we stopped and I stood for a moment admiring the view. "Look, you can see the whole town from here. Over there's the pool!" Marian said.

And the graveyard, I thought to myself and then hurried to help Marian unload the cooler onto a picnic table.

Dr. James stuck her head out of the car window. "All set?"

Marian nodded.

"All right. I'll pick you up at eleven o'clock."

"But, Mom. It only starts at nine. That's too early."

"Marian, we discussed all that and we decided." Dr. James drove off, leaving Marian looking unhappy.

She continued watching her mother's car until it disappeared down the hill. "Did you hear from Jeff?" she asked then.

"No. He must be at a friend's house, maybe a sleepover. There weren't any lights on at his house."

Marian frowned. "Somehow I don't think he has any friends."

The smell of chlorine floated past again, bothersome and annoying. "I'll check on him tomorrow if we can't find out anything from Ryan when he gets here." The chlorine scent was gone now. "C'mon. You should at least have a good time while you can," I suggested, tugging at her elbow.

Kids were piling up branches and firewood. Rose was there, some girls I'd seen hanging around the pool, and a bunch of guys I didn't know, plus Shannon and Sean, the lifesaving weight lifter. Where were Leech and Ryan?

I scanned around but didn't see them. An older kid with a Youth Department T-shirt strummed on a guitar, another one lit the fire. Marian and I stood by it for a few moments, watching the flames lick around the kindling. When the bigger logs caught and blazed, it was so hot we backed away. Finding a couple of stumps, we sat down within the growing circle of kids, some of whom were singing along with the guitar.

"You thirsty?" I asked Marian, feeling the fire hot on my face.

"Yeah, you?"

"Yeah. Stay here. I'll bring the cooler over." I walked back to where we'd unloaded it and as I hoisted up the metal box, there was Shannon. "Oh, hi," I said softly. She seemed alone now. "Do you want a Coke?" I asked hopefully.

"Sure, that'd be nice." She smiled.

I opened the cooler and handed her a cold can. "Come sit with us." I motioned back to where Marian waited, just as Sean returned.

"Let's move our lawn chairs closer to Marian over there," Shannon told him.

He looked me over for a moment, probably remembering when he'd escorted me out of the pool. Then he strolled over to the other side of the campfire, grabbed a lawn chair in each fist and carried them over to our stumps.

I opened my bag of chips and offered him some, trying to show Shannon just how mature I could be. Sean grabbed the bag, stuffed his face and passed the rest around the circle.

Shannon hadn't even noticed. She sat up in her chair, stretched her neck and looked around, frowning. "They aren't anywhere, Sean," she said, standing up and strolling to the other end of the hill. Shading her eyes with her hand and peering toward the graveyard, she twisted her mouth thoughtfully. "Do you think they're at the pool already? I can't understand why they aren't here."

"What's that?" Sean sounded peeved as he followed after her. "Relax," he said, placing his hands on her shoulders. "They're a pain. Be glad they're somewhere else."

"I can't relax." Shannon paced away from him. "Can we just go down and check?"

Sean shut his eyes for a second and then slapped his hands together in exasperation. "How many times tonight? They couldn't have drunk enough beer. Just sit down!"

Shannon gave him a sharp look and continued pacing.

The sun sank completely behind the horizon and twilight softened the view from the hill. I watched as she stopped for a moment to chew the nail down on her baby finger then I turned to stare at the fire. A small, quick sound from inside me made me look up suddenly.

The sky turned from purple to black and the largest moon I'd ever seen came out and lit up the night. The noise! There it was again, this time louder and longer.

A crash! Shards tinkling. Was it inside my head only? I looked around to see if anyone else reacted to it. No one did. It didn't matter because just as suddenly I knew where Leech and Ryan must be.

20

"Marian, I have to go."

"Well, there's no bathroom, we just go behind the bushes."

"No, no! I have to go back. I forgot. The police were going to keep a special watch on Mrs. Dobroski's house while she was in the hospital. But she was supposed to be out today."

"How are you going to get there? My mother won't be back till eleven."

"Is there a phone somewhere?" I glanced around, looking for an outdoor telephone booth somewhere among the picnic tables.

"Down the hill, back at the park entrance," Marian answered.

"Forget it. I don't have time to wait for someone to come and pick me up anyway."

"You're going back alone?"

"You see anyone here who wants to come with me?" Kids were sitting closer to the fire now, singing and laughing. Shannon was roasting a marshmallow with Sean.

Marian folded her arms and frowned. "I will."

She made me smile. I knew it was hard for her to leave the party. And even harder for her to be brave. "Thanks, but no thanks. I'll go back, check on the house and alert the police that Mrs. Dobroski's not home. If everything's okay I should be back in an hour."

"What if you're not?"

I frowned. "If I'm not, go to the phone booth and call my house."

"Are you in the phone book?"

"Not yet. Shoot! Do you have a pen?"

She shook her head. "Just tell me, Nicholas. I can remember, I know I can."

"All right," I sighed, looking at her pleading face. As if believing in her was such a difficult thing. "Five, five, five, nine, four, four, one."

"Five, five, five, nine, four, four, one," she repeated, with her eyes rolling up to help the effort.

"Okay, I'm going. See you later."

She nodded. "Hurry back, Nicholas."

"I will." I jogged lightly down a path but gravity helped speed me up. At one point I stumbled over the root of a tree. Ouch! My ninety-dollar jeans had a hole in the knee.

I started running again. How could I have been so stupid? I thought, as my feet pounded the ground. Ryan only wanted me to go to the party so I wouldn't be at Mrs. Dobroski's when he and Leech broke in. I figured it would be at least a half-hour walk so I ran a little faster. At Main Street, I needed to make a decision. Should I cut through the cemetery?

It would save a few minutes' time. I looked over the graveyard. The tombstones cast long shadows in the moonlight, the gatehouse at their head looked like a silent conductor. And then I heard someone crying. It sounded like a baby — or at least a very upset child — but at the same time it had a distinctly unhuman tone. As I approached Alexander Gresko's grave, the cry became louder and at increasing intervals. Then I saw her. Small and white, sitting at attention near the stone door, loudly telling the world that she was a lioness.

"Misha! What's wrong?"

She cried again and shifted as though she wanted to approach me but thought it might be abandoning her post. "How did you get out anyway?" I noticed something sparkling in Misha's fur and stooped to examine her. Glass.

My stomach turned upside-down. Quickly, I scooped up Misha and ran the rest of the way to Mrs. Dobroski's house, looking toward the window with a sickening certainty. It was broken. On the ground, a million more pieces of glass sparkled in the moonlight. The back door stood open and I rushed in, scanning the room for missing objects.

The bargain basement radio from the counter was

gone. My eyes looked upward to the top of the fridge. It looked oddly empty.

The soup tureen! It was missing! "Rosenthal China, very expensive and precious." Mrs. Dobroski's words came back to me, too late. What should I do now? *Don't bother about the window and don't follow them!* Her warning echoed in my head. I put Misha down and picked up the phone. It was one of those strange, old black models with a rotary dial. The first time I stuck my finger into a number slot I slid the dial to the wrong number. It took a few tries before I reached the police station.

"Is Officer Vellenga there?" I asked.

"I think you're in luck. She just stepped in to start her shift. Let me pass you through."

I heard someone pick up.

"Officer Vellenga here."

"It's me, Nicholas. I'm at Mrs. Dobroski's house. They've broken in."

"Nicholas! Are you sure they're out of the house? You shouldn't have gone in. You might have been hurt."

"They're gone all right."

"Good. I want you to stay put till I get there. Don't try chasing them or anything foolish. Do you understand?"

"Yes, Ma'am."

"All right. I'll be there within ten minutes."

I placed the receiver back into the cradle.

And then I smelled chlorine, subtle at first. The scent drew me to the back window again. And then the smell became stronger. I looked out the hole that had been glass before. The glowing figure stood in the graveyard, the chlorine odor overpowering now. *Stop him! Hurry! Before it's too late!* The message echoed loudly in my brain.

Don't bother about the window and don't follow them. Mrs. Dobroski's words from the hospital. *Stay put till I get there.* Officer Vellenga's.

Stop him!

I said it out loud as that thought won over the others. I dashed out the back door to the fence and climbed over it. I needed to run to him to find out the answer. When I drew closer, though, Sasha faded away. I began to live the nightmare.

Or was I asleep? The moon lit up the tombstones so that they seemed to glow. The stone gatehouse loomed up ahead. My legs pumped hard beneath me and my lungs burned with every breath. *Hawh, hawh, hawh.* My heart became a hammer, pounding rhythmically against my ribs. Between the fire and the pounding, I thought my chest would explode.

Faster!

All other thoughts left me. Faster! I didn't think more speed was possible but I felt adrenalin shooting through me.

I made it to the gatehouse. Be careful!

As had happened in my nightmares, McNamara leapt out at me. You have to stop him! I sidestepped McNamara but he lunged for me, grabbing some of my shirt. I tried to tug away but his grip was strong.

Suddenly a demon scream made us both freeze for a split second. A body of white fur sprang between us and my shirt tore as I pulled away again. Misha! Stumbling over her, McNamara lost his grip and this time I broke away. Still he was only a heartbeat behind me; I needed to do something.

In my mind I heard the rustling of paper and an incessant drone. I looked up at the wasps' nest and shuddered. Then I took a deep breath and jumped up like a basketball player trying to touch the net. My fist knocked the nest straight into McNamara's face.

I didn't even look back to see what effect it had. Now everything I had needed to go into my legs. Bending them, stretching them, larger and faster strides. The chlorine smell burned at my nostrils. Where was I going? Faster and faster, through the gate around the corner. Almost there.

Loud voices spoke from the other side of the pool fence. Leech and Ryan. I could see Ryan on the diving board, bouncing up and down.

"Stop!" I screamed. Ryan looked my way and then down into the water.

"Oh my God! Jeff!" he yelled.

I ran into the pool area and ripped off my sneakers. I dove into the water. For a moment, I couldn't see anything. Where is he, where, where? I felt my way along the bottom. I touched something soft and cold.

And then the moon shifted position and I could see him clearly. He was lying face-down, the movement of the displaced water making a lock of his hair wave. He looked dead, but I couldn't take the time to panic. Snatching one of Jeff's wrists, I dragged him up and up. It took a hundred years and when I got him to the surface, I quickly blew into his mouth. It was too late. Jeff's body felt cold and limp and his skin looked grey.

"He's dead," Ryan cried out. "Oh my God, he's dead."

"It can't be too late!" a voice yelled out in agony. It was my voice and yet it wasn't my words. Sasha!

Leech helped me out of the water with Jeff. "Get help!" I gasped at him and he took off.

"My father was supposed to be watching him! I didn't even see Jeff come in. He looks just like that body." Ryan wept hysterically.

I gently turned Jeff over and tilted back his head, pulling at his chin and nose to open his mouth. Then I blew a quick puff of air into him, looked at his chest and felt his neck for a pulse. Still nothing!

Tracing down his ribcage to locate it, I placed the heel of my hand over his heart. I thought back to the lifesaving practice Marian and I had seen, and pumped, counting. One and two and three and four and five, and then puff into his mouth. Again! One and two and three and four and five, and puff. Don't stop! I heard Sasha's voice inside my head. It can't be too late!

Only sobbing came from Ryan now. He'd knelt down with his hands covering his head. Give up and cry; it's what I wanted to do too, I was already so tired. One and two and three and four and five. Puff!

I felt the pool water rolling down my skin with my sweat and wanted to wipe it away. But I couldn't interrupt my rhythm. One and two and three and four and five, and puff! Every second counted.

Jeff's chest didn't rise, he still wasn't breathing. It

was all going to be for nothing. I could never keep it up. Was I even doing it right?

"Nicholas!" Marian's voice called out from somewhere.

"Help me, Marian. Help me!"

She quickly knelt down at Jeff's head and counted with me. "One and two and three and four and five." Marian took over breathing into Jeff's mouth.

"One and two and three and four and five."

"Nick! What's happening? Did anyone call an ambulance?" Vaguely somewhere in the back of my head this voice registered as Shannon's.

But I didn't answer. Just as before I focused everything into running, now every ounce of me was pushing down on Jeff's heart. "Come on, Jeff. Come on." Over and over.

"Son, you can stop now. I'm getting a pulse." A man in a grey uniform knelt in front of me. A woman pulled me away from Jeff. I sobbed and struggled with her.

"It's all right. It's over now," she told me in a soft voice. I noticed the stretcher beside Jeff. "You may have saved the boy's life."

May. His skin still looked grey and now his face was half-covered with an oxygen mask.

The attendants loaded Jeff's body into the ambulance and Ryan jumped in behind the stretcher. Just before the doors slammed he whispered the last couple of words I wanted to hear right then.

21

"Get Dad," he said weakly.

I collapsed on the ground, shuddering. Sorrow, pain, regret. Not only my own — I felt it doubly strong. For a little boy who drowned ten years ago. And another fourteen year old, who died before he could save his friend.

But I couldn't help any of them right now. I couldn't change or stop the course of history. All I could do was one last thing for Jeff and his brother — find their father.

I picked myself up and pushed Marian away. "I have to find him, Marian."

She shook her head. "You're not going alone this time."

I sucked in a ragged breath and found no energy left to fight. "Fine. Come on," I said and staggered back toward the graveyard.

When we saw the Fairchild truck parked close to the gatehouse, I broke into a run. My sides hurt but I called out as it pulled away, "Wait! Wait!"

No use. "Marian, go back to Mrs. Dobroski's. See if the police are there. I'm going to the store."

Marian nodded and tore off. But I couldn't run anymore. I made it to the bus stop and leaned against the signpost.

A bus pulled up after a few minutes. "You're not coming in here to throw up, are you?" the driver asked.

I shook my head, climbed on and flung the change into the slot. Then I just stood there gripping the bar.

Fairchild's Treasures looked dark as the bus pulled into the curb, but I spotted the truck in the alleyway beside it.

"Open up," I yelled, and pounded on the glass door. No one answered so I jiggled the doorknob and pounded again. One heavy, frustrated whap and the glass shattered around my hand. My wrist stung and blood ran down my arm as I stepped through the door into the darkness.

"Hold it right there."

A light snapped on and Fairchild stood behind the counter, a gun in his hand.

I stopped and stood perfectly still. "Where's McNamara?" I asked.

Fairchild put the gun down. "He's not . . . here."

A rustling sound and a movement in the back room told me he was lying.

I stepped toward the counter, calling, "Mr. McNamara?" Fairchild didn't stop me so I kept walking. "You have to come out. Jeff fell into the pool." Still no response. "We're not sure he's going to make it." I walked behind the counter. "Ryan needs you at the hospital."

"You're lying. I left Jeff asleep." McNamara moved into the light now too.

"He must have been pretending." I looked at Fairchild. "Just the way Corey used to."

His mouth wavered. That slight quiver in his lips gave me courage.

"I tried to save Jeff just like Sasha tried to save Corey."

"What do you know?" Fairchild asked. "Alexander let Corey drown. That's what that delinquent did."

I shook my head. "No. McNamara did that."

Fairchild turned to McNamara now. "What's he talking about?"

"Ah, he's blowing hot air. He doesn't know anything," McNamara said lightly. But his eyes couldn't meet Fairchild's. Instead they locked on to mine. "Shut up, why don't you?"

"I can't. Jeff and Ryan need you. You have to come to the hospital," I told him, but my words only made him look angrier. One last thing — and I couldn't do it. Was it all for nothing? Had history repeated itself with no change at all? And then I spotted something in the back that changed my mind.

222

Dobroski's soup tureen. An antique Fairchild couldn't resist.

At least I could prove McNamara and Fairchild were involved in this break-in. And if I could do that so easily, I thought I should try for more. Maybe then Sasha could finally find his peace. So I focused on Fairchild. "Did you know Eric Fallows found Sasha's wallet near the gatehouse in the graveyard?"

Fairchild shrugged. "So what? Gresko got what he deserved." But Fairchild looked ruffled — he hadn't known.

"Mrs. Dobroski saw McNamara slam Sasha against the wall. Ryan even saw the body."

Fairchild raised his voice, as though loudness could push back the truth. "You don't understand. Corey counted on Gresko and he didn't show." Now his voice broke and Fairchild spoke quietly. "He left my son alone to drown. Gresko's death was simple justice."

"No, it wasn't. McNamara murdered Sasha in the graveyard before he could get to Corey. If he hadn't, Corey would still be alive today."

"He's lying. Don't listen to him!" McNamara sputtered, turning an angry red. He was losing it and I decided to push him over the edge.

"Is Mrs. Dobroski lying too? She heard the grandfather clock chime just before Sasha left her house. She saw you hit him. If you don't believe me, believe Mrs. Dobro —"

McNamara choked off my words before I could finish, lifting me by my shirt collar. The room stood on it's side for a second and I felt a strange lightness.

From somewhere I heard the crunch of glass and Officer Vellenga's voice as McNamara slammed me against the wall.

"Let him go!"

22

"I've stopped him, I've finally stopped him," I sighed as I collapsed on the couch after Officer Vellenga left. "But it's too late for Jeff."

Mom put a blanket around me and from that moment I started to shiver uncontrollably. "Oh God, oh God," I kept repeating.

"Give him something warm to drink and then let's get him to bed." Where had Dr. James come from?

Dad actually picked me up to carry me upstairs to bed. I felt too high from the ground, too dizzy; I wanted to be sick. And then I was lying in my bed.

In my haze, I felt soft, gentle hands on my shoulders, pulling me up. I thought for a moment how nothing could be so wonderful, so soothing as those soft, gentle hands. "Nicholas, here." Mom's voice.

I wanted to leap up and hug her and be hugged till everything was better again but I had trouble enough sitting up.

"Drink this." Mom gave me a sip of something fiery.

I sputtered.

"It's brandy. It'll warm you," she explained.

There was a strange moment when I nearly laughed. Earlier I had to promise her I wouldn't drink at a bush party, now here she was plying me with liquor. I swallowed a little more. "How is he?" I had to force myself to ask, I was so afraid of the answer.

"We don't know, Nicholas. Just rest."

"No, no, no!" I tossed in my bed. "I can't just put him out of my mind. I can't sleep!" The person I wanted to hug a few seconds ago, I wanted to shake now. "It might work for you, Mom, but I just can't do that."

One of her soft, gentle hands touched mine and I felt ashamed. "Nicholas. I'll stay awake. The hospital will call."

But if it was bad news she'd never tell me. It might upset me too much — it wouldn't help matters any.

Mom *must* have sensed what I was thinking. "Nicholas, I promise. The moment I get any news . . . any news," she repeated, "I'll wake you."

I looked into her eyes and saw truth in them.

"You know, it's funny. These past couple of weeks, I kept dreaming about you swimming. I didn't know what it meant."

"You too, huh?" I laughed. All the last weeks of irritation washed away and I felt our old friendship return. I shook my head and my whole body began to tremble again.

"Here, have a little more brandy."

I sipped and then said, "Could you tell Dr. James that Marian helped? Without her I couldn't have kept up the CPR. Marian knew what to do."

"The attendants told her already."

"Mom, she got Officer Vellenga for me too."

Mom nodded.

I burrowed under the covers. Nothing could warm me. Mom piled two sleeping bags on top of me and then made some tea. After that, despite everything that had happened, I fell into a dreamless sleep.

"Nicholas, Nicholas!" Someone called my name from far away. Now someone shook me. "Jeff regained consciousness. He's going to be all right!"

He's going to be all right. The thought warmed my whole body and a grin broke across my face before I even opened my eyes.

"They're keeping him in the hospital a couple of days for observation while they try to locate his mom. Nicholas?"

I was still grinning. "I'm fine," I told her as I hugged her.

When she finally left the room, I smelled chlorine again. This time soft and gentle. In my mind I could hear the laughter of a young boy. I stood up and walked to my window.

Sasha stood at the end of the yard, not moving,

only waiting. Seeing him this time I didn't feel pain, or sorrow or regret. I felt a deep, warm peace. After a few minutes, I saw a smaller figure appear beside him. Then the laughter and the chlorine smell faded as the two of them walked away, hand in hand.